We dedicate this issue to
Sunila Abeysekera
(1952–2013)

"When everyone is criticizing you, then you are doing the right thing."*

Sunila Abeysekera was a Sri Lankan feminist and human rights activist, internationally known for decrying the injustices and atrocities committed, especially against civilians, during the long war between the government of Sri Lanka and the Liberation Tigers of Tamil Eelam (LTTE), as well as in its aftermath. While a Sinhalese, and thus a member of Sri Lanka's ethnic majority,

Sunila demanded that all perpetrators, regardless of ethnicity or political ideology, be held accountable. Her position often found her at odds with the government, and she spent periods of time outside the country when the risk became too great. But she never ceased to be outspoken. Her work was widely recognized and included awards from the United Nations and Human Rights Watch. Sunila cofounded or was associated with several women's rights groups and initiatives, locally, regionally, and internationally. She had worked as a singer, dancer, actress and drama critic and was a lesbian and a single mother, parenting both biological and adopted children. Her life inspired many other feminists, lesbians and human rights advocates internationally, as well as younger people active in progressive politics in Sri Lanka.

*UNESCO Courier, September 1999

TABLE OF CONTENTS

NOTES FOR A MAGAZINE

"Living as a lesbian is still a dangerous business in many parts of the world[.]" Those are difficult words to confront, and behind those words are painful, lonely, hostile, and brutal realities about lesbian lives. In my previous "Notes for a Magazine," often I have written about celebration, joy, and rejuvenation for lesbian culture. Yet *Sinister Wisdom* is equally about confronting, with open eyes and open hearts, the challenges that face lesbians—and all beings—in the world.

I cannot imagine two writers, organizers, and intellectuals more well suited to guide us through this important journey of looking at, thinking about, and comprehending life when living as a lesbian is still a dangerous proposition. This issue excavates both what living as a lesbian means and what exile means. Exile, a condition and experience that separates self from self, self from family, self from community, self from country, contains, expands, and complicates sexuality and lesbianism. The rich material gathered in this issue of *Sinister Wisdom* considers many facets of exile and its fractured, resilient, and complicated relationship to identity.

Joan Nestle and Yasmin Tambiah are two giants in lesbian culture and letters. When Joan told me that she and Yasmin wanted to guest-edit an issue of *Sinister Wisdom*, my heart fluttered, my mind engaged, and I said yes. Immediately.

Many readers know Joan Nestle through her work as an activist, author, and editor. Joan was one of the founders of the Lesbian Herstory Archives in 1975 with her then partner Deborah Edel. For many years, the Lesbian Herstory Archives was housed in the apartment she shared with Edel in New York. It was there that her long-lasting relationship with *Sinister Wisdom* began, as she welcomed each issue into the collection. In her nine authored and co-edited books, Joan has kept alive the layers of her history, from the queer bar days of the '50s through the lesbian-feminist movement days of the last part of the twentieth century and now from the perspective of a seventy-four-year-old fem lesbian woman who lives far from her beginnings. Having Joan as a co-editor of a special issue of *Sinister Wisdom* is an extraordinary honor for the journal—and a treat for all of our readers.

Yasmin's research interests focus on questions thrown up at the meeting points of gender, law, and sexuality in postcolonial contexts and where militarization configures sexuality. Yasmin, however, is not only a visionary researcher but also a gifted writer. I first encountered Yasmin's creative work in *Conditions*. In "The Civil War," published in *Conditions: Seventeen* (1990), Yasmin describes her experiences in Sri Lanka, "Those at risk cannot afford ignorance. I have learnt to recognize the languages of domination. I gather a community of resistance for a dangerous, yet necessary, journey toward radical transformations." (p. 102.) Yasmin brings a fierceness and a tenderness to her work as a writer, scholar, and editor. I believe you will feel the strength and vision of both Yasmin and Joan on every page of this issue. I thank them both for their work.

A brief word about the business of *Sinister Wisdom*. Welcome and thank you to the thirty-six new subscribers to *Sinister Wisdom* who joined during our Spring Subscriber Campaign. I will repeat the campaign in the spring of 2015. In the meantime, encourage your friends to subscribe! In April and May of 2015, I would like to add thirty-nine new subscribers, to celebrate our thirty-ninth year of publishing, but encourage your friends, lovers, comrades, and co-conspirators to subscribe at any time.

As you read this, *Sinister Wisdom* will be in the thick of our fall fund-raising campaign. I hope you will take a moment to read about it at www.SinisterWisdom.org. I have an incredible publishing plan for 2015, but I can only do it with your financial support. If you are able, please make a charitable gift to support *Sinister Wisdom* before the year ends.

Finally, I appreciate your time, support, and passion for *Sinister Wisdom*. I hope I am matching and exceeding the community's passion for *Sinister Wisdom* in my stewardship of the journal.

In Sisterhood,
Julie R. Enszer, PhD
October 2014

NOTES FOR A SPECIAL ISSUE

We met over twenty years ago at the first literary awards night of the Astraea Lesbian Foundation. At the time we were both living in the United States. In 2003 we talked about working on an anthology, "Questions of Home: Lesbians and Exile," but the publisher we approached was not interested in the topic. Joan was in Australia by then, and Yasmin was based in Sri Lanka but travelling widely for work. Yasmin communicated with Joan about the consequences of the war between the government of Sri Lanka and the Liberation Tigers of Tamil Eelam (the LTTE), and the fallout on Tamils in the country as well as on people of other ethnic groups. Yasmin later moved to live in Australia, where her family had sought refuge as a consequence of the war. When the opportunity arose for us to be guest editors for *Sinister Wisdom*, it provided a way to revisit the theme of lesbians and exile which had remained pressing for us both.

While collecting the material for this issue, some key points struck us. Living as a lesbian is still a dangerous business in many parts of the world, especially when lesbian lives become enmeshed in agendas of national purification that make scapegoats of lesbians and nonconformists more broadly. In other instances, simply being a lesbian is not necessarily the most pressing issue in one's daily life. This is particularly true if a lesbian lives in, or is closely connected with, war zones, whether such zones result from armed conflict within or across national boundaries or from violence experienced in a socially and economically marginalized community. However, being a lesbian informs and complicates the responses to, and survival strategies developed in, such contexts. Thus the stories lesbians tell are marked by the crisscrossings of all their histories.

Sometimes the experience of exile needs to be strategically claimed, even as a means to resist that very state.

It is impossible, therefore, to talk about exile without invoking politics.

We decided to provoke questions about the utility and limits of the term *exile* by including a spectrum of other processes and states of dislocation, displacement, eviction, illegitimacy, and rejection. These states cannot be considered without simultaneously foregrounding acts of dissent, resistance, and transformations, and always from a lesbian perspective or on a lesbian continuum. For instance, how do we think about bodies of difference—bodies marked by ageing, different abilities, sex, or gender? How does a lesbian negotiate the contradictory demands imposed by male-centered nationalism that denies her existence and her desire for agency to create new kinds of community? What stories will a lesbian refugee tell, and who will listen? How does the movement towards national centers, as symbolized by campaigns for marriage and the right to serve in the military, restructure notions of belonging—and the consequent creation of new outlaws, new exiles?

We are grateful to *Sinister Wisdom* for giving us the freedom to explore such issues. We would like to thank Joanna Cattonar and Dianne Otto for their editorial assistance.

Joan Nestle
Yasmin Tambiah
Fall 2013

REPORTAGE: MY EXPERIENCE
ON MAY 17, 2013, IDAHO DAY, IN TBILISI*

Mariam Gagoshashvili

Sunday, May 19, 2013 at 8:59 p.m.

On May 17, IDAHO day, I was together with twenty other activists (eighteen women and two men) when counterprotestors attacked us. We were surrounded by police who were in turn surrounded by a large number of counterprotestors. Even though their number was increasing and aggression from them was growing, swearing at us and spitting in our faces, the police were repeatedly telling us to leave and to de-escalate the situation. We obviously did not want to leave because the aggressive crowd would attack us even more. Needless to say, we did not engage in verbal contact with the aggressors. We stood still. Some of us were demanding that the police take special measures to protect us and we requested some transport. However, they were reluctant to provide this. We were trying to get hold of three contact persons provided by the Ministry of Internal Affairs, but with no success.

Later, two women representatives of the United Nations joined us. They showed their work ID to police, and only after realizing that UN representatives were with us did the police take some steps. With the guidance of UN staff members, they led us to the entrance way of a residential building where we found temporary shelter. On the way to the entrance, several of us were attacked by counterprotestors who threw stones and plastic bottles filled with water at us with full force. One of the girls had a head wound that was bleeding. Police did see clearly who was throwing stones but did not do much. As far as I could see, nobody got detained by the police.

We spent some time in the shelter, where the UN representatives urged police to take measures. I believe that thanks to their efforts, police provided one yellow minibus for our evacuation. They made a corridor and we were evacuated from the building. Two policemen accompanied us into the minibus while the aggressive crowd tried to reach us, throwing stones, spitting, and cursing us.

The crowd was preventing the minibus from leaving. They attacked us from outside, broke windows, grabbed our hair and bodies, threw bottles, and tried to drag us out of the broken windows. The minibus was moving very slowly because of the crowd and because its front windows were damaged. The driver couldn't see. Some people tried to get into the minibus and they kept trying to drag the driver out. The two policemen did a good job ensuring that the minibus did not stop. I am grateful to them as well as to the driver.

We were taken outside Tbilisi to a safe place. Members of our group were safely delivered home or to nearby streets by police patrol cars.

As a result of this attack, one activist had head wounds, two activists had concussions, others had bruises, cuts, and torn clothes. Everybody was shocked and devastated.

With full credibility, I can say that the crowd that gathered against us was more than ready to kill us. Minutes longer in the minibus would have been our end.

*IDAHO is the International Day against Homophobia and Transphobia. Tbilisi is the capital of Georgia (Eurasia).

YOU ASK METO TELLYOU ABOUT EXILE

Samar Habib

Y ou ask me to tell you about exile.
You say *come let us have a look deep into the Freudian wound and see how this woman is made up.*

She is all wires, entangled in veins and nerve endings that lead to a heart which says *I speak, you listen. I don't take orders from you, brain.* But now, I listen, you say *write!* and in spite of itself, the heart acquiesces.

The first exile must be the moment we are expelled from our maker's womb. To this day, I have yet to meet someone who does not know this first exile. But we make a home for ourselves in the false autonomy of self and we meet our maker, usually, here on earth. From this moment forward we begin to die, that is, we begin to discover identities thrust upon us and the identities we wittingly or unknowingly construct for ourselves.

The ancient mystics insist that in this false autonomy of self we gain ourselves at the expense of all there is. They say that we begin to identify with a thought-generating machine, a ceaseless random noisemaker that tricks us into thinking this is who we are. The ancient mystics sit under trees for years, sometimes decades, trying to dispel the illusion of self. And then they tell us they are happier this way. That this is the true path to the actual enlightenment. It was never the discovery of the scientific method, they say. And I might never have believed them had it not been for the "Buddha Boy" in Nepal, who was filmed continuously for an excess of eighty hours, sitting under a tree, eyes closed, not moving, not eating, not drinking, not getting up to relieve himself. The locals say he sat there for three years, disappearing every few months for a while and then returning, and once he burst into flames. When he came out of his trance his message seemed terribly simple. If we don't stop being such assholes to each other, our world will come to an end. I could have told you that, without sitting under a tree. But Buddha Boy must really know exile at the very moment he is able to reach oneness with being, because at some point he must return to us, to see what poor buddhas we make.

Existential nihilism really knows exile. Foucault, too, when he tells us that all things are constructions of the mind, when he negates so brilliantly the very notion of the a priori, he sends us into exile, the exile of infinite subjectivities, that only those who have been institutionalized like him can know. The very victims of the invention of madness. So too does Friedrich Nietzsche know exile. We make everything up. There is no center. At the very least, we're not it.

I am trying to remember my second exile. I am trying to decide whether the love of my family and the sanctuary of the home they provided to me in my childhood was enough to ward off the exilic feelings of a gender atypical child in the ruthless classroom that relished Catholic corporal punishment. I think the sanctuary of the family home was indeed enough, because I was yet destined to learn what my gender and sexuality would come to mean, both in the context of my cultural heritage and in the conveniently, outwardly decorated, "protective," "democratic" West.

I don't know which number exile this one is, but I do know that it was a recent one. I was hit by a train. I was naïve enough to think that I had the freedom to be a homosexual—it was, after all, the twenty-first century. I could be gay and a scholar, I had academic freedom to think, and there were laws to protect me from discrimination. If the impact of the collision were not so painful, I might laugh at the ready innocence with which I believed in the veneer of civilization. And maybe if I were a white girl, talking about white things, maybe, just maybe, they would have hit the brakes and tried to lighten the impact a little. But since I was a homosexual of the Palestinian persuasion and neither my own people nor the owners of whiteland have any interest in the actual existence of someone like me, since unfortunately I derail so much of their mythologies about themselves and each other, there was no need to hit the brake.

I don't know why you want me to revisit all this pain. Did I tell you that I am reluctant to announce what I see? That from experience, I know everything I say can and will be used against me? That it suffices to have an accusation directed toward you, regardless of its veracity— that the mere conjuring of the specter of an accusation functions almost identically to actual guilt?

Where do I begin with disentangling the myriads of exile that seem to be my fate? Shall we start with the most familiar and accessible account of collective trauma? Shall we begin with the "dirty" word *Palestine*? Shall we begin with a Palestinian born into a Lebanese exile that was deemed too distasteful to be the subject of dinner conversations and classroom wonderings in the innards of Western Sydney? Nothing can send you further into exile as much as the ignorance of the magnitude of suffering that the cells of your body have inherited. The dead were silenced by murderous warplanes and then Mahmoud Darwish gave them a voice, and I carried that voice with me into the lecture theatre, and when the university management excised Darwish's Memory for Forgetfulness, it managed to kill the dead another time, to throw another vacuum bomb in their midst. And this is why I imploded, because inside me was a vacuum that went off, because I saw the veneer of civilization shatter before my very naked eyes. Why did you silence the dead again? Have they no right to speak? Have they no right to have their stories heard? Don't you see, there is no such thing as a war crime, that *war* is the crime?

I realized that in the eyes of the world, not simply my own, I shall always be a Palestinian, no matter which passport I hold. I went to San Francisco so I could be a gay Arab and discovered a liberal arts bubble that cherished what I had to teach about all that was queer in my oceanic Arabo-Islamic civilization. But even in San Francisco the pale face of ignorance managed to take hope away from me. It took the bureaucrat three minutes, three minutes to decide the course of my life. So I went right back to where I started—to the original scene of the crime, to the city of my first dreams—Beirut. Here, life is a veritable chaos. For the last few months there has been no government, a practical civil war rages in the far north, an armed militia sends its boys to die in Syria, traffic lights that no one heeds, footpaths reserved for anything but pedestrians, electrical outages, water shortages, salt water wells, concentration camps, ridiculously cheap cigarettes and an exponentially growing face of poverty on the streets. Suddenly, I find myself having to profess my Christianity, though I have never been particularly religious and I know far more about Islam. Everyone in this country is an exile and yet I do feel at home, perhaps because being back here alleviates the survivor guilt I felt in the neat streets of whitetown.

I am surrounded by people of infinite talent that time has forgotten, that god never bothered to grace with the opportunity to exercise their creativity. Either poverty or their condition of ongoing statelessness has sucked the joy of life out of them. If I were to imagine their Ayurvedic natal charts, there would be some blockage in their rising sign that would prevent them from the blossoming that they so richly deserve. I think of all the great minds of this and the previous generation, something I have no doubt Allen Ginsberg observed,[1] who were buried under the weight of menial labor, just trying to survive. And I think of all the poems they wrote that we shall never read, the paintings we shall never see, the inventions we shall never discover, the books we shall never write or films we shall never see about them. I am in good company here. I am not any better than any of these people. Why should I lament my own annihilation when far greater minds have met with far worse fates than mine?

I distinctly remember the moment I rediscovered my cultural heritage and my right to a place within it. For so long I had been

---

1 "Yes, I saw the best minds of my generation destroyed by madness...." *Howl and Other Poems*. San Francisco: City Lights Books, 1956.

told and made to believe that my gender and sexual orientation were western inventions. That it would not be possible for me to be myself had I been a true Arab. I had forgotten the photograph taken when I was nine years old, in war-torn Beirut, never having seen, heard of or even known what a "lesbian" let alone a "western invention" was. A photo that captures me standing, suave, hands in pockets, wearing a grey and white checkered suit, with a proper tie. I had been made to forget that photo, to ignore the evident nativity of my gender and sexual orientations in relation to all around me. Even if they were just constructs, which I do not believe, these were constructed here, they were made in Lebanon, by a Palestinian child in the privacy of a few cubic centimeters that make up the self. I owned them, those so-called constructions: my Arabness owned those so-called fabrications, and there was never any dispute in those early days. I don't know if it was Foucault who had me convinced that I didn't really exist. I think I had misread him as many do. But there was a moment very early in my research career, when I was a graduate student, and I was listening to Abd el Halim. That was a revelation. "Why do you blame me," he sang "if only you saw how beautiful his eyes are, you'd say that my preoccupation and late nights are not too much for him." I was theoretically literate in the culture enough to know that the "he" of the poem was supposed to be read as a female beloved in the mainstream. Abd el Halim was not supposed to be singing about another man. But the universality of that kind of love, for which we have no equivalent word in English, 'ishq, enables the beloved to also be of a universal gender. "He" to me was a woman, and "he" to a man in love with another man was that other man. "He" was a floating signifier expressing a freewheeling soufi boundlessness that encompassed the whole of human experience of passionate love in all and any of its configurations. Sitting at my desk, chipping away at a doctoral thesis, letter by letter, word by word, sentence by sentence, I felt myself return to a home from which I had been forcibly ejected. I returned to and within my very

Arab body. I glimpsed a reality past cultural constructions of self, I lost the decenteredness of the poststructuralist critique of reality itself. I glimpsed the end of exile and the nihilism shimmered, and melted momentarily. I knew then that home really is where the heart is, that union with the beloved—whether material or abstract—banishes exile.

LETTER TO IGBALLE ROGOVA: NOTES ABOUT LESBIAN BODIES IN OUR DIFFERENT HETERO NATION STATES

Lepa Mladjenovic

*D*raga Igballa, Dear Igballe,

Kosova 2.0 [on-line progressive journal][1] asked me to write an essay on my lesbian life and I decided to take this opportunity to write an open letter to you. You are my dear lesbian friend and also my first knowledge of Kosova.[2] You are my precious Amazon buddy from 1995 when I first saw you in black solid shoes. All throughout the years of war we kept close without many words, learning from one of our favorite lesbians, Audre Lorde who wrote in *Our Dead Behind Us: It is not our differences that divide us. It is our inability to recognize, accept and celebrate those differences.* I wish to remember together with you some of the stories of our dyke lives in the 1990s. You worked with rural women as a feminist activist in Prishtina [the capital of Kosova] in the midst of the Serbian occupation, while I worked with women survivors of male violence as a feminist activist and as a member of Woman in Black against the Serbian regime in Belgrade.

First I must tell you where I am now. O dear Igballica, my dear Igballinka! I can say I am in the Capital of the Lesbian and Gay

---

1 http://www.kosovotwopointzero.com/en/article/935/the-sex-issue-one-year-later-the-debate-is-more-important-than-the-attack.

2 Editor's question to Lepa: What spelling of Kosovo should we use—in your letter you use Kosova, in Igballe's letter that follows, she uses Kosovo. Lepa's answer: "You see, we have to decide what to do. In the Albanian language, it is named 'Kosova,' and I am deliberately using the Albanian naming, even though it is not so known here nor anywhere. Otherwise officially it is 'Kosovo'—but this is the Serbian way to name it! And in the UN and EU it is Kosovo. Therefore, the old Serbian naming becomes the official naming. The aggressor's name becomes the generic name. So—what do you say?" The editors have decided on Kosova.

Photo Credit: TKTK

Igballe Rogova (left) and Lepa Mladjenovic

Mecca in the United State – Provincetown, Massachusetts, a small place on the ocean across from Boston where lesbians and gays have concentrated for decades. The nature here is wonderful, but there is something else which is exceptional. For the past fifty years this has been a place where first artists, gays, and lesbians came and visited, and then many others moved here because of the freedom and the caring community. I encountered so many good people here. I can't believe it! In fact I realized that I have never had enough of a social or political supportive environment to be able even to dream that such a place could possibly exist for real: where many women walk hand in hand, gay men too, lesbian families play with their kids, gay fathers carry babies, while rainbow-peace flags are waving and welcoming us all around town. My friend Michelle, a lifelong dyke who moved here eighteen years ago because of her trust in the community, says she never locks her door. The town has around three thousand citizens and in the summer about thirty thousand visitors. Same-sex marriage has been legal in the state of Massachusetts since 2004. Here are some images:

Two lesbians are walking toward me. One pushes a baby carriage with twins. I wave to the kids and all four smile and wave back to me!

By the ocean a wooden veranda with the sound of music . . . I see one middle-aged gay guy, looks almost like Elton John alone there. He's singing out loud with the music, and then he takes his dog and starts dancing with him and kissing him facing the sunshine! Touched by this sight, I thought, if men would dance with their dogs with such joy, there would never be any wars again!

I enter a small shop, there is a cashier near the door, a lovely middle-aged lesbian standing there with a beaming smile who greets me Hello. I feel like a lightning rod has hit me in the heart! In embarrassment, I look around and go out. What touched me so much? First of all, I felt her self-confidence, the calmness, the warm ease of her lesbian body. I had a feeling of the fullness of her balance with herself and with her surroundings. She also looked like an owner of this shop. Excellent, I thought, she once made a decision to move to this town and work where everyone would be at ease with her as she is. I was thinking further: not only does she love herself being a lesbian, but her community sees her as a lesbian too. I felt her body energy full of not only the tenderness of her lover's caresses but also the care of her supportive neighbors. No wonder I trembled. I think again: I was never before in a place where lesbians can be surrounded by each other and the friendliness of society. Such a liberated power of her body can be experienced by a lesbian who is surrounded by social and political freedom. Then I thought how I feel my body more present and alive to me in this town—I'm walking down the streets conscious that I am being seen by lesbians. This pure fact inspires my body with a special erotic energy. Being among lesbians is a different form of existence.

II

Here I am, thinking about this letter, dear Igballe. Are you drinking coffee now? I have my green tea and dark chocolate to feast with you. I know you don't like sweets, but *ajvar*[3] and cheese.

The first images that came to me were those from the women's parties that you organized a few times in Prishtina in the middle of the low-intensity war[4] of the Serbian regime against Albanian citizens in Kosova. Was it 1997 or so? Usually the first day, we would be out in a restaurant whose owner you knew—a safe place therefore—and we would be with women friends and your sisters.

The second night, we would be in your home. I remember in those days your partner Rachel Wareham, you, and me—one day we three got the idea to celebrate C-Day! Yes, if Eve Ensler could invent a V-Vagina Day, we could invent a C-Clitoris Day! And so you organized all-women parties around Christmas. You were dancing hot oriental dances and those that you do with a glass full of wine on your head, which you told me only men do in Kosova! Those were fantastic parties, we would talk lesbian stories, open lesbian gifts gently packed with care to each other, smoke nonstop, and drink. I remember I would come back to Belgrade excited and friends would ask me *Where have you been?* and I would say *An all-women party in Prishtina!*, and they would say *Where?* in total surprise, and I would repeat, *Prishtina!* No, they did not understand it. But I was proud. I was proud of you, of our feminist gang, lesbians in revolt from Belgrade, Prishtina, Budapest, New York—for we knew that women dancing is political.

---

3 Lepa: "I am smiling. 'Ajvar' is a sauce/paste made of red paprika, very special for the Balkans. It would have been the best way to explain it if we could have eaten it all together."

4 Editor: "What do you mean by your phrase, 'low-intensity war'? This sounds like a contradictory phrase. Lepa: "During the 1990s before the bombing and before the shooting, Milosevic had all different fascist methods of oppressing Albanian citizens, many of which were invisible. But the Serbian regime had all the power and Albanians could not behave freely, such as sing in Albanian, get passports, be employed, travel, and other losses of everyday life. But all of this was not official and there were no formal killings so we, members of Women in Black and other people on the Left, named it 'a low-intensity war' before anyone called it a war, before the 1999 war.

One of the first times we walked down the streets of Prishtina, I was glad to be with you and your friends and I said, *Let's sing some of the Albanian songs!* And you told me: *To sing in Albanian on the street! What are you talking about! You must be mad!!* I will never forget it. No, I was not mad, I was totally ignorant! I did not yet know how deeply and vastly the Serbian regime was contaminating and controlling every segment of your lives in those years. I could not imagine that you could not sing in your language in your own town! And more so I thought that none of my friends in Belgrade know this! The Serbian regime was controlling media, so ordinary citizens in Serbia in those days were not supposed to know that Albanian citizens in Kosova were denied entry to the Serbian state Serbian institutions, that Albanian children went to private dark cellars meant as schools, that health exams were done often in cellars too, that the majority of your people were expelled from work, and that Serbian terror was affecting all dimensions of everyday life, day and night. As Hanna Arendt has said clearly in *The Origins of Totalitarianism*: *totalitarianism has discovered a means of dominating and terrorizing human beings from within.*

III

I remember once in those years around 1997 you drove to Prishtina and I was sitting on the seat next to you. All of a sudden you were not relaxed any more. You turned off the music. I did not have a clue what had happened. I said, *What's going on?* You said, *Silent, please!* Your body was trembling. Only a few minutes later would I learn that we were passing the Serbian police checkpoint to enter Kosova. That day I felt the fear in your body to the end of my bones. I froze. I will never forget it. Your fear was deep and cold as iron, re-forming your body into a protective fortress and a mind concentrating on vigilance.

The images of Serbian police threatening Albanian citizens were coming back to my mind. Your story of cruel humiliation when you were asked to come back to the Serbian police station every day at 8 a.m. to pick up your passport, three years after your request. They would let you wait in an empty old room until 2 p.m. Then, in a threatening voice, they would tell you to come back tomorrow. And so on for twenty-two days, while in reality your passport was in the drawer in the room right next door. In feminist theory we call these "acts of nonsense," and they are known as the pattern of violence in families, as well as in totalitarian regimes and in concentration camps. Making citizens exhausted and humiliated by "acts of nonsense" I remember in the war in Bosnia and Herzegovina in the nineties many times Serbian soldiers demanded Bosniak men eat grass in front of them. In the genocide in Burma, women who were imprisoned testified that they were ordered to eat flies.

In your car that day, still silent, I was thinking that in fact I don't know how many sleepless nights you and your family must have encountered in those years of fear. And this was still before the war of 1999. I could have not imagined, because the fear in your body was a new matter for me. I'd never felt you this way before. This was a huge difference between me and you. Adrienne Rich says *The moment when a feeling enters the body / is political.* How true this is! Imagine, I always thought this moment of fear in the car separated us. I was uneasy and thinking what is my responsibility in this situation? When there are two who belong to oppressed and oppressor—then one has a task. One way to observe identities is to search the history of their pain.

In another day in those same nineties I was supposed to give something to an Albanian friend of a friend from Prishtina, so I went to a bus station to give it to him, a book I think. We were sitting in a small cafe in the bus station and he was talking in a low voice, so that I could hardly hear him. I noticed all of a sudden that it was a very skilful low voice. He knew techniques I had never encountered before; many ways to speak in this low voice so that the others nearby in the public space would not hear him.

There is a feminist book that Alice Schwartzer, a feminist writer from Germany, wrote many years ago, *The Little Difference and Its Huge Consequences*, where she describes gender oppression as *the little difference*. That's this *little difference* between you and me, dear Igballe, the history of Albanian bodies during the Serbian regime of terror. For example, me and my brother: we lived in the same family, in the same street, but I had a fear of rape and my hetero brother did not. My fear teaches me to walk the streetlights side of streets at night, while he, as a fear-free man in this particular situation, can wander any street side or any street by night. I am here opening the theme of how different identities— being oppressed as Albanian, as a woman, as a lesbian—imply sets of different emotions that await us in certain historical moments. When, with my Roma friend, I want to enter the park in Belgrade where skinheads hang around, she tells me *No, I'm not going there!* Her fear tells her to avoid the place where racists have already attacked Roma women before. I ask myself: how do we learn about each other's feelings? Because if you know that I am aware of how you feel, I'm the witness of your pain—you have a chance to feel less alone. Also, I am then not alone because I have knowledge of your pain inside my body. This encounter of two friends with different imprints of social pain is what inspires me in this letter to you, dear Igballe.

IV

Remember when you all invited me and our dyke-feminist friend, Bobana Macanovic, to come to the First Human Rights Conference in Prishtina in December 1999? It was after the war had been stopped by the Kumanovo agreement, and finally Albanians could rest a bit from decades of Serbian rule over Albanian citizens. By that time, it was already clear that the Serbian regime during the war of 1999 had expelled by force and terror close to 850,000 Albanian citizens from their homes. Also, by that time we already knew that more than eleven thousand deaths in Kosova had been reported to the International Criminal Tribunal for the former Yugoslavia. This is almost twice as many dead in Kosova as in the Second World War. On the other side, after the Kumanovo Agreement, thousands of Serb citizens were forced to leave Kosova: of the almost forty-five thousand Serbs and Roma people in Prishtina, only about four hundred remained.

The first ever Kosovar human rights conference was to be held on the tenth of December 1999. Bobana and I decided to go, but we did not really know how to get to the border where our friend waited for us on the Kosova side. After the war of 1999, there were no more buses from Belgrade to Prishtina. Not one. So we took a bus to the last village in Serbia, and then we walked. This was the last year of Milosevic's police. We did not have a clue how to behave on this new border. We waited in front of the police barn, and one of the policemen said: *Where are you going*? I said *To Prishtina*, and he said *Over there, how come?* He sounded as if he were standing on the border at the end of the world, saying there is nothing else over there. *All people are gone out of Prishtina, and you are going in?* This sounded as if there were no more people in Prishtina at all. *What are you doing there?* he asked. I remember I felt a wave of fear; what shall I tell him, what the hell are we doing in Prishtina? We had planned to not say that we were going to the human rights conference, but on a private visit, just to be sure we got to see you all. So when he asked this question the second time I said, *My boyfriend is in Prishtina.* All was understood and he said *All right, go.*

On the other side of the KFOR (The Kosovo Force—a NATO-led international peacekeeping force in Kosovo) international border, we had the most elegant activist, our dear friend Nazlie Bala, waiting for us in a black shining car, and an international police jeep following us all the time. Many different things happened in the next three days. Bobana was afraid to speak Serbian on the streets of Prishtina, so the deal was to speak in English, but she did not really know much of it. In those three days we slept in your flat, we spoke Serbian only in there, in order to respect the pain of the neighbors. Bobana and I heard appalling stories of women who were expelled from their homes in Kosova, like you and your family, afraid, squeezed into trains that recalled the train deportations to Auschwitz, robbed of ID documents, spat at in the face, thrown out on the Macedonian or Albanian border to wait days and nights. We heard also stories of the pain of women who throughout the 1999 wartime remained at home under the Serbian terror of daily intimidation, sexual violence, and death threats. So many details of profound humiliation.

At the conference, I was perceived as "a Serbian body," and this I took as my specific responsibility. I listened as a sister and at the same time I knew this was an encounter of "Sisters from Serbia" and "Albanian sisters from Kosova." The stories I heard moved me to tears, to the edge of disgust and rage. Crimes done in my name, by men from my streets, by men with uniforms with the same national emblem as on my passport, played out with my money. Only a few years after the genocide in 1995 in Srebrenica! Again.

After this complex experience in Prishtina, I came back with two crucial issues in my body and on my mind. First, I could not get away from the pain I have felt from the Kosova war, and could not stop thinking what must I do? Is expressing my feeling of deep sorrow enough? What is my responsibility as a feminist activist from Serbia? As a Woman in Black how to act upon the shameful crimes done to the Albanian people? What kind of apologies for the crimes done in my name can you hear with trust? These questions stayed in me and many of us activists for all the years to follow as we carried on in pursuit of a feminist approach to transitional justice.

After I wrote my report from this conference, I realized I had a hurt in my belly from another issue. It came to me suddenly: How could I lie to that regime policeman on that border about my boyfriend? In order to overcome obstacles I did not follow my lesbian heart, or my political vision. How many times before have

I had to hide myself? Lesbian life in lesbophobic society implies constant lying. To remain merely alive, lesbians in a patriarchal setting have to lie at some point in their lives. We all become liars. I know that. But this time I said OK, I've done it, fine, but that's enough. After this border event I promised myself not to disguise my lesbian self ever again. No fascist border, no war police, no check point will make me do this again. Ah, I feel relief writing this for the first time now. Dear Igballe, thank you for listening. I know you will understand me. We are all in this misogynist world, and as activists end up trapped in some places because we fear, but we do the best we can in given circumstances to survive. And then we learn. We say, OK this is it! And we move on! I love you dearly my buddy, I can only imagine how many times you were torn between your "Albanian body" and your "Lesbian body" in your life.

And then we cry sometime, alone or near our lovers, because we know we must compromise, even if we don't want to. For lesbians in the war zone this is a constant dilemma. Palestinian lesbians told us their dramatic stories on this theme as well. This is an issue for lesbians even without the war: how to synchronize the ethnic family on one side and lesbian lovers moon-sisters on the other. Muslim, Chicana, Afro, Asian . . . I will never stop talking about how much I admire you for that capacity and softness with which you care about your family and your lesbian community at the same time. I can't wait for the next dance with you. And, just to remind you that you are loved among feminists in the entire region: *If Igballe makes the party, we're gonna dance until dawn!* May the sunshine kiss your face today, dear Igballe.

~ Lepa, your Bukurije[5]
Provincetown, Massachusetts
October 2012

---

5 Lepa: 'Bukurije' means beautiful in Albanian because my name 'Lepa' means beautiful in Serbian, so Igballe named me this way.

LOVE BEYOND BORDERS:
A LETTER TO LEPA, MY FEMINIST MENTOR

Igballe Rogova

Dear Lepa, *Draga Lepa,*

I was also asked to write about being among the first persons out as a lesbian in Kosovo. For more than a month, I've had an inner struggle: what to write?

I have this image to uphold as the first woman to marry a woman in the former Yugoslavia. You attended our wedding in 1996, remember? My then partner Rachel wore a crown of flowers and a dress. I wore pants. We danced in the rain with such joy, as any couple on their wedding day.

But those whom I once considered friends in Kosovo twisted our beautiful story. I want to write openly to Kosovo 2.0 about the hypocrisy of these self-proclaimed "human rights activists" and journalists who forget human rights when it comes to homosexuality. They wrote slanderous false information, calling our wedding an orgy in the rain. They nearly ruined what should have been among the happiest moments of my life. Cold shoulders and solemn stares greeted Rachel and me when we returned to Kosovo, rather than smiles and congratulations.

Only with support from my family was I able to stand strong against this prejudice. If my family hadn't supported me in 1996, perhaps I would not have been able be here today like so many gays and lesbians who have had to seek acceptance outside of Kosovo. This led me to consider writing about my family, and how important family support is for LGBT persons.

However, dear Lepa, I am still uncomfortable sharing these stories. Today in Kosovo we still have a homophobic media who seeks to sensationalize us. I fear that people may misuse my stories. Amid my inner battle on how to express myself to the skeptical, to the slanderous, to the curious, to any reader who would read my words, I received your letter.

I read your letter a dozen times, and every time I felt emotional. You reminded me of the bittersweet 1990s: the struggles we had in Kosovo and our precious moments together. I felt inspired to write a response to you. I cannot say in two pages what you mean to me and to the women's movement in Kosovo, but I will tell two important stories.

I remember the solid black shoes we both wore the night we met. It was 1995, and my first visit to Belgrade. Julie Mertus, a professor from the USA, was writing a book about women's experiences of war in Kosovo, Serbia, and Bosnia. She told me women activists in Belgrade go in the street every week to protest against the policies of the Milosevic regime. I didn't believe her. I thought all of Serbia was against us. But Julie was persistent. She made me curious, and I had to see for myself.

We went by bus, and I was extremely uncomfortable. Here I was, a Kosovar Albanian, going to the heart of the beast—Belgrade— the place from which Milosevic orchestrated his horrible human rights abuses. "Why am I going to Belgrade when Kosovars are going through hell?" I sat with second thoughts and guilt. Then, *bam!*, the bus tire exploded.

While waiting outside the bus, Julie started making conversation. "You have such a beautiful family," she said.

"What?" I didn't understand.

"You, Janet, and her son."

"Oh, noooo," I said. "Janet is just a friend, a roommate. We're not together."

But Julie's question made me think. Perhaps, I could speak with her about the feelings I'd had for some time. "I mean . . . yes," I continued. "I've kissed a woman, but I was confused." Julie was the first person I told about my sexuality. Along the road to Belgrade, she encouraged me to accept the feelings I had. She told me that many people around the world have similar feelings and even relationships, that women could live together as a family.

When we arrived at my first Women in Black meeting, I sat next to you with my big black solid shoes. I remember clearly your first words: "Mmm , butch shoes." I looked at you, probably with a blank stare. "What's butch?" I thought to myself. I'd never heard the word before. I didn't respond. It was my first meeting with Serb women in Belgrade. I didn't know you. I didn't trust you.

Then we went to the protest. I did not participate, but sat to the side to study Serbian women's actions. I wanted to see if what Julie said was true. Indeed: you stood in the street with banners against Milosevic, against the war in Bosnia and Herzegovina, even against Milosevic's acts in Kosovo, like the closing of Albanian language schools. The banner that touched me most read, "Albanian Women are Our Sisters."

Some of the people passing by were angry; they swore and yelled at us. Others called us "Rugova's bitches," after the leader of Kosovar Albanians' peaceful resistance, Ibrahim Rugova. But you stood strong, as you have every Wednesday since the war started in Bosnia in 1992. Every week you stood there for an hour in silence while your bodies spoke out against the war.

I will never forget the moment when a man came and spat on you. I saw his saliva slide slowly down the side of your face. You did not move. If it had happened to me, I would have taken my hand from the banner and cleaned my face. But you were strong. With your body you told that man, "You do not exist. I am here protesting with my body against what is happening, and you cannot stop me, even with your spit."

It was at that moment that I clicked with you, dear Lepa. You showed me a model of an activist in action. Until that day, action involved yelling. You showed me that sometimes the body speaks louder than words. Years later, when five thousand women stood in silence in front of the U.S. Cultural Center (which served as the U.S. Embassy) in Kosovo in 1998, you inspired our idea to stand still with a white sheet: one side represented peace and the other side was blank, illustrating that as Albanians we had no rights, so we had nothing to write.

You became my feminist mentor, Lepa. You gave me great books: Audre Lorde, Alice Walker, Angela Davis. You taught me methods of standing against oppression and not to hate all Serbs, but to hate the Serb regime.

That night after my first Women in Black protest, I came to your party. The room held a mixture of old and new friends, mostly lesbians. At first, I was nervous. I was drinking and watching others. A special space was created there, where lesbian sisters could dance freely.

But try telling this to my Kosovo readers. Many will not understand. They will equate lesbianism with sex, not solidarity. They will think we had naked orgies. They somehow cannot comprehend that Love and Sex are not the same thing. Do heterosexual people jump on each other every time they meet? No. Nor were women jumping on each other that night. Women were simply dancing, happy, safe, free.

After two hours, I realized, "This is my family. This is where I belong." At that moment, for the first time in my life, I accepted myself for who I was. "*Bingo*! I'm a lesbian." I finally realized what the feelings I had inside of me meant. I felt an expulsion of joy, and I danced like I had never danced before. My body felt liberated from the confusion I'd felt for so many years. I returned to Kosovo a different person. I felt liberated . . . *free.*

How strange, though, to say that I felt liberated in Belgrade. It was (and for many Kosovar Albanians still is) the epicenter of all evil: the roots of the regime that had stripped us of our rights. Even today, dear Lepa, I hesitate to reveal to readers that this spectacular moment in my personal history happened in Belgrade.

Why? Do you know what people here said after the war? "Internationals brought homosexuality to Kosovo," they said. "Internationals converted Kosovars to gays and lesbians." I know it is hilarious, but such stupidity remains here today, Lepa. These same people say that Belgrade as "the root of the regime and all evil" influenced me to become a lesbian, which they evidently consider another form of evil, forgetting that lesbianism involves love, not war.

In any case, those who would attribute my lesbianism to a Belgrade conversion would be wrong. It was not only that night. It was the bus tire blowing. It was Julie making a space for me to talk about my feelings and explaining to me what butch means. It was the magic I felt when I first kissed a woman in 1994, but didn't know why. It is the solidarity that I felt in a room full of women who accepted me for who I was . . . who I am.

This was the same solidarity that existed with my sisters and friends in safe spaces in basements during the 1990s, when you visited us. It is the feeling of Provincetown. Your tales of Provincetown give me hope that one day we may live in a world where solidarity comes before the homophobia that stifled my feelings for so many years.

Oh, I have such mixed emotions remembering that time, dear Lepa.

I remember 1999. As NATO's bombs fell, you called me every night. You begged me, "Leave now. I know what happened in Bosnia. Serbs will hit even harder because of the NATO bombing. They will want revenge. You cannot trust even your Serbian neighbor." You were so right.

There you were, a Serb woman in Belgrade whom I had just met, trying to protect me. Then there was my Serbian neighbor whom I had known all my life. I grew up playing with her sons. Since I received my first salary in 1984, I gave her money because my father taught us to give to those in need. Amidst the bombing, when we Albanians could not buy anything, even bread, I went to ask her if I could give her money for cigarettes. Soon after, she, the woman I had helped all my life, informed the police that our family was still at home, hiding.

The police came with guns, pushed us out of the house, marched us to the train station, made us wait in the cold March rain for hours, shoved us onto trains like cattle and threatened to burn us alive, before forcing us to walk along land-mined tracks to "no-man's land" between Kosovo and Macedonia. We became refugees.

Even as refugees ourselves, we activists worked with the more than forty thousand refugees in the Cegrane camp in Macedonia. You came to visit. You couldn't say you were Lepa from Belgrade, so you introduced yourself as Maria from Italy. It meant so much to us activists that you had come.

And here we are today, dear Lepa, thirteen years after the war. You still stand strong in the streets of Belgrade with your placard. As Kosovo negotiates with Serbia, we women will stand in solidarity, ask our governments and the world, "Where is justice?" Where is the justice for what the police did to me and my family; for what we saw my Serbian neighbor steal from our house? Where is justice for Kosovar Albanians' lost pensions? Where is justice for the women who were raped, the thousands who were murdered, the families of the still missing persons? You were the first woman from Serbia to sign our petition, demanding justice for these crimes committed by the Serbian regime. You stand by us today in solidarity, dear Lepa.

Now some might say my letter is political. It is. Our bodies are also political. Our sexuality is political, whether we want it to be or not. Indeed life is political, isn't it, Lepa? And I can only dream that one day our politics here will be like those in Provincetown, where people greet us equally regardless of gender, ethnicity, or sexuality.

I will never forget what you have done for the people of Kosovo and for me, my butch buddy, my feminist mentor, my soul-sister, my Bukurije.

Your Igo
Prishtina, Kosovo, September 2012

Note: These letters were published in a slightly different form in the on-line KOSOVO 2.0 Sex Issue, December 2012, a ground breaking event which made possible the first public discussion of sexual differences in Kosovo for young people. We want to thank Besa Luci, the editor of the magazine, for giving us permission to use parts of the letters. To celebrate the launching of the issue, Lepa and Igo were invited to read their letters to a gathering of over a hundred young people in Prishtina, but a group of men, intent on breaking up the event and despite some police presence, rushed the room and smashed chairs and tables as well as sculptures of the human body. As Lepa wrote on December 15, 2012, "It was supposed to send us a message of threat and to scare all, especially as these were young people organizing the event, lots of young women and men. But the feminist organizer of the event quieted the room after the men had left by saying now it was clear how the personal is political." Lepa and Igo finished their reading to great applause.

THIRTIETH

Yasmin Tambiah

Between formulating responses to a research assistant on the "Asian Century," straightening laundry to catch a winter sun, complimenting my partner's sartorial choices for work, it insinuates itself. Not sly like a mouse nabbing rice grains in a New Haven pantry, or startling like an elephant stepping out from scrub on the road to Minneriya. Just present. Always. At times as at the small end looking reverse through a telescope, at times at middle distance, at times as near and as wide as this parched continent at world's end where I never imagined I'd live. And especially today.

Today my father's people would begin to be erased. Today my family would know their disinheritance. Today in England, after an ecstatic university year, I would learn the terms of leaving. Thirty years ago. Today.

And I have learned well. The iterations: restlessness, no committed dwelling, no heavy furniture (although the movers debate the weight of books). Movement is permanence; permanence is alien; permanent alien.

There was a point of departure.

There is no point of return.

24 July 2013, Sydney, Australia

---

*July 24, 1983: "Black July," the anti-Tamil pogrom that is remembered as the beginning of the twenty-six-year war between the government of Sri Lanka and the forces of Tamil nationalism.

RETURNING MY NATIONALITY TO YOU

khulud khamis

Come to think of it
ultimately—
my (your)
nationality
is just an empty shell
i used to think—
i
need to belong to.

But,
and since—
you (us)
do not (cannot)
ever—
see
me—
as one of
you (us)

Therefore—
I
out of my own—
free
will

give it back

And instead—
i

choose
to be a—
citizen of the world.

Unshackled by—
belonging
nor by
that
word become
dirty—
called
nationality.

LOST IN TRANSLATION

khulud khamis

parts of my identity
have
been-
for some (un)identifiable

reason
lost in translation.

Floating between-
the languages
in a-
void
between the-
continents.

THERE IS NO PLACE FOR US

Xi'an Glynn

I am a stranger in my own home. This was once a place for us and now it is just a place. Once here and now vanished in space like ancient relics of the motherland. Removed and replaced, displaced, and dishevelled. There is no mitigation through this silent arbitration. Our frustration is discussed in living rooms where there isn't enough room to live. And we discuss whether or not it is relevant to forgive this simultaneous influx and exodus.

I keep hearing stories of the invisible. We are and have always been the true aboriginals, and sadly I imagine a day when a person of African descent in New York City is a novelty and rarity because of the scarcity of the most precious resource—land. The National Black Theater, The Apollo, Langston Hughes Way, Frederick Douglass and Malcolm X Boulevard, The Harlem State Building, the Savoy and the Cotton Club, and the list goes on and on. The rent gets higher and higher.

I keep hearing stories of displaced Brooklyn residents and the gentrification of the South Bronx and wonder, will this be me? Uprooted? Cast away like a pariah? Held a victim to the unnecessary commerce of space? Manhattan was purchased for twenty-four dollars. Brownstones in Harlem are selling for two million. You do the math. There will be an aftermath.

Police are paid to stop car after car with black and Latino faces, and we are silent as homes are turned over because breadwinners are doing time. And those bread winners were lucky because they were the few to find work. These prisoners have homes that are stripped away when income is lost because of an arrest and lawyers' fees and penalties for just being black.

I am a stranger in my own home and you know this is crazy when the European even wants a part of the African ghettos. This just proves that we were already rich and always have been. We let this precious land slip away like water slipping through our hands. We move out of these rich cultural enclaves wanting something more when all that we ever wanted was right there in front of us all of the time. We complain about the piss in the stairwell, the broken elevators, and the lack of heat in the winter while someone is ready to move into our neighborhoods. Like they say, someone's garbage is another man's treasure. It's time we start appreciating what we have and investing in our home communities before we will have no home. Until then, there is no place for us.

3'OURBEH[1]

Ghaida Moussa

Make room for that which may or may not come.

Sweep each corner,
        awakening dust that fell in love with settling
        and forgot how to fly.

Scrub windows of layers between you and your heart,
                                so you may see.
Open them.
            Release suffering that is eager to speak.
            Release pain that is no longer useful.
            Release aches that remain nameless.

Burn life into the air,
        and watch it fall in the places you've crafted for it,
        in case it were to appear
        in a feeling.

Carry it with you when it leaves you,
                and make room;
                for what leaves is always only
                in process of
                returning.

Make room for that which is in process of returning.

---

1 3'ourbeh is a difficult word to translate from the Arabic. It can mean stranger, estrangement, foreignness, Other, but it is also used to explain the process of becoming a stranger to your home, to be expatriated, exiled.

TAZAKAR[2]

Ghaida Moussa

May you remember
    in each tongue roll,
    in each hint of the aroma of coffee,
    in each carton of figs,
    in each sight of rain in August;

May you remember
    every time you hold the spine of a book,
    every time you pass a woman with oversized hands,
    every time you climb a hill that makes your calves burn,
    every time your hair reaches for the humidity in the air;

May you remember
    as the breeze of summer nights makes you pull your
    blanket under your chin,

    as you eat with your hands,
    as you drink in celebration;

May you remember
    if your heart loses its *inaam*,[3]
    if your spine loses its *qiwa*,[4]
    if your eyes lose their *lotf*;[5]

May you remember
    if you forget to remember.

---

2 "To remember" in Arabic.
3 "Grace" in Arabic.
4 "Strength" in Arabic.
5 "Kindness" in Arabic.

LESBIANS WHO SPEAK BEYOND THE PALE: THE EXILING OF DISSENT*

Joan Nestle

Dedicated to the Pussy Riot Women: Nadezhda Tolokonnikova, Maria Alyokhina, and Yekaterina Samutsevich

Here in Melbourne, Australia, I walk down a worn footpath almost every morning, a street that reaches from Moonee Ponds in the west to Sydney Road in the north. I walk to get pain out of my bones and to think, think as I pass by the old wooden houses of Italian, Lebanese, Greek, and Vietnamese migrants. My walk turns when I reach the railroad line right before the Brunswick Baths, a community gathering place where toddlers splash in the wading pool and older Calabrian women gather in the *acqua profonda*, delighting in their weightlessness. Dawson Street is very far from my Broadway walks of so many years ago, but these last days I have occupied two geographies at once, or even more, as those whose horizons change late in life often do. I am looking for a way to pull all the materials of my thinking together, all the turn and toss of unexpected understandings, of painful clashes of identities, of unacceptable political realities. I have lived with shifting expulsions from the center of things for a long time, both within my lesbian-feminist community and from the larger American society, but I am haunted now by these new divisions, these new called-for silences.

I sometimes come late to New York news stories here on the southern rim of the Pacific, and so I had not read the lengthy report about what had happened at New York's LGBTI Center in 2011 when its directors decided to ban groups and events

* With gratitude always to La Professoressa, Di Otto, who has opened the world to me.

deemed too controversial, but I had seen the broken rainbow logo, with a tear dripping from the fissure at its center. In times of heightened national certainties, where one can easily be seen as betraying the national or community narrative, these cracks, these ruptures of false unities, are precious terrains. We become larger than ourselves; our intersectionalities, our histories all worn on the same body, now catapult us beyond our queer community borders. As Pauline Park wrote in coverage of the events, "The Israel/Palestinian Conflict Breaks Out at the NYC LGBT Community Center." For two years, the center barred any discussion of Israel and Palestine within its walls, walls that had seemed so expansive in the 1980s and 1990s, now shrunken by the demands of national orthodoxies. As I write these words, I am reminded of the theatrical "Padlock Law" passed by the New York State legislature, in response to the lesbian-themed play *The Captive*, which outlawed any depiction of homosexual characters on the New York stage from 1927 to 1967. Yes, we carry histories.

"If one cannot voice an objection to violence done by the Israeli State without attracting the charge of anti-Semitism, then the charge works to circumscribe the publicly acceptable domain of speech. It also works to immunize Israeli violence against critique by refusing to countenance the integrity of the claims made against that violence. One is threatened with the label, 'anti-Semitic' in the same way that within the US, to oppose the most recent U.S. wars earns one the label of 'traitor,' or 'terrorist sympathizer,' or indeed, 'treasonous.' These threats...seek to control political behavior by imposing unbearable, stigmatized modes of identification" (Judith Butler, *Precarious Life: The Powers of Mourning and Violence*, Verso Books, New York, 2004).

In 2013 the center went too far when it banned Sarah Schulman, one of America's most prolific and enduring lesbian creative artists, from speaking about her book, *Israel/Palestine and the Queer International*. What words would she say that were too unspeakable to hear in the Keith Harding decorated building? That Palestinian bodies were as deserving of life, of a hopeful future, as Israeli bodies, that actions needed to be taken, that her recent meetings in Palestine and Israel with queer Palestinian and Israeli anti-occupation activists as well as her history in America made clear that Israel's occupation of Palestine has created an apartheid state calling for international sanctions and boycotts to end its illegal and brutal use of state power? A lesbian writer making sense of her own life in a new way, challenging us to listen: "One of the strangest things about willful ignorance regarding Israel and Palestine is how often 'progressive' people like myself, with histories of community activism and awareness, engage in it" (Sarah Schulman, *Israel/Palestine and the Queer International*, Duke University Press, North Carolina, 2012). This time the center could not hold its position, and in June 2013 the director issued a statement: it had lifted a ban on the writer whom they had barred from speaking because of her subject matter.

It seems my American life—lived as a queer, Jew, fem lesbian, feminist—has been bracketed by national fear campaigns that call for heightened surveillance and punishment of dissent. I entered the 1950s as a ten-year-old and left the decade as a politically active twenty-year-old in McCarthy America. To be queer meant to be a subversive, an American pariah, to be the focus of state surveillance. "Perverts Called Government Peril: They Are as Dangerous as Reds" (*New York Times*, April 19, 1950). We now know that in the late 1950s the FBI was sending undercover agents into the meeting sites of Daughters of Bilitis (DOB) and the Mattachine Society. On other pages I have written about the thought- and life-killing tyrannies of the House Un-American Activities Committee (HUAC), its choke hold on dissent. In these years the New York Times carried articles about the nest of homosexuals in the federal government. In 2011, the following language was used by Michael

Lucas, an influential gay man, when the center allowed Queers Against Israeli Apartheid to hold its meeting there: "As I always believed, the LGBT Center of New York is an anti-Israeli nest" (Pauline Park, "Israel/Palestinian Conflict Breaks Out at the LGBT Community Center," 2011/03, p. 20). After a threat to mobilize a defunding campaign against the center, permission to allow the group to meet was rescinded.

I have been following the closing down of public discourse which questions the legitimacy of the Israeli occupation here in Australia and in America for several years now, such as the firing of teachers who held unwanted opinions, the closing of debate, the stigmatizing of anti-Occupation public figures, the canceling of films, the picketing and protesting of lesbian writers who have spoken out, such as Judith Butler and Jasbir Puar, whose work and person have been ridiculed and defamed for showing the links between gay and lesbian sexual rights and the Israel-Palestine conflict. But I was stopped in my tracks by all that was happening in the heart of New York's gay community.

At seventy three, I have seen the reasons for communal and national banishment shift under the pressure of global struggles for power. In what may be the closing decade of my life, new ironies, new heartbreaks have emerged but the effect is the same: hyper surveillance of the feared other and accusations of treachery hurled at those who raise dissenting voices. Dissent gives birth to invectives, the marking of a turncoat, the spit of hatred. "The LGBT 'queers' had threatened to storm or 'surge' into the Center if they did not receive official approval for their group meeting. 'Surging' and 'storming,' Arab street mob behavior is a vision and a tactic that reminds me of Nazi Brownshirt behavior. Think Kristallnacht" (Phyllis Chesler, "NYC Queers for Jihad," *Front Page Mag*, May 30, 2011). Here in the words of a longtime feminist, history loses meaning. Never have I felt the conflict of identities as deeply as I do now, now when the circle of American acceptance has widened to include its right-thinking queers. Another way to put this:

never have I seen so clearly the manipulated offers of inclusion, the seduction of our difference—all we have to do is join in the hatred of the national enemy. For the Jewish lesbian, this bargain includes accepting the special relationship between America and Israel, accepting in silence the suffering of the Palestinian people both within Israel and in the occupied territories of Palestine.

"The terms of degeneracy have shifted such that homosexuality is no longer a priori excluded from nationalist formations" (Jasbir K. Puar, *Terrorist Assemblages: Homonationalism in Queer Times,* Duke University Press, North Carolina, 2007).

As we have said in the Notes to this issue, the editors are aware that the prevailing view is that lesbians have always been in a state of exile; decades of marginality prove this. To be a lesbian, we often said, is to resist the state. But what if the state has a vested interest in telling us who to hate? What if the state offers us money for our film and literary festivals, for our pride marches, for our centers, for our political support? What if the state holds out a passport to the center of things by granting marriage rights and unfettered military service? What if the state says join us in national agendas of banishment and you will be part of the nation? To be anti-Palestinian, to promote hateful oversimplifications of Muslims and Islam, to pretend queer Muslims do not exist, to support Israel no matter what codes of international law it chooses to ignore because like America, it occupies an exceptional place in today's fear-filled world? What if we partner with national whiteness and exile brown bodies whose cultural heritages fall outside what is deemed safe? What if we accept the rule of consumer-corporate economies and in so doing come to agree with the state about which lives deserve to be lived in dignity and which deaths are not to be mourned, which bodies must be protected and which can be allowed, indeed, required to be broken under state-sponsored torture? Will we not change our lesbian selves so long used to seeing resistance in our touch, in our culture, in our feminist politics into something else—a wanted national self who is welcomed into her walled home?

As I was writing these pages, a Facebook message came to me about a newly released anthology, the first ever, of transgendered and gender queer poetry called, *Troubling the Line* (T. C. Tolbert and Time Trace Peterson, ed., Nightboat Books, New York, 2013). Troubling the line is exactly what dissenters do. What we thought we knew or who we are is falling apart. We must ponder who we are now. In Europe, the far right has created a new united front—Geert Wilders, a Dutch gay man who supports gay marriage and Israel's right of occupation embraces Marine Le Penn, the darling daughter of the French right whose agenda is antigay and neutral on Israel, both agreeing that their common enemies are the migrants, the refugees, the Muslims, the Romany people who threaten "their way of life." In America, more and more, many who should know better are moving to the right and the Right, knowing better, is beginning to endorse gay marriage and gay candidates. All my senses—lesbian, queer, Jew, old—tell me that if we do not trouble the line of xenophobia now, that if we accept all in the name of being an unquestioning friend of Israel or a supporter of gay marriage or a good capitalist, that if we do not see clearly the suffering of those we have condemned to endless war or endless curtailment of hope, we become partners with a new world order that will have a very narrow sense of who is human.

Yes, I walk streets that lead to different horizons now, I have fewer and fewer long known contexts, but in this unanchored time of my life I have met many lesbians—Palestinian, Israeli, Serbian, American, Croatian, Bosnian-Herzegovinian, Romany, Sri Lankan, Australian, Indian—who are troubling the lines of fervent nationalisms, who are refusing to stay in their ordained national place, who use public stance and public speech to question abusive national powers, who know dangerous bargains when they see one, who have danced on the altars of punishing regimes. Courage and determination to question, to find the evidence of the unacceptable and the brutal and to make it known, this for me now is how we give meaning to the word *lesbian*.

A DIFFERENT KIND OF EXILE

gracepoore

When my mother died in 2000 in Malaysia, I realized that she was the closest thing to a homeland for me. She was place, time, memory, sentiment, and I felt cheated of what might have been if she had outlived my father. It was not until after her death that I understood how much I had been yearning to go home to her without him. When my father died six years after my mother, I was travelling for work. I had no inkling, no sense of his death for ten days, while I had dreamt of my mother's death two weeks before the telephone rang in my Silver Spring apartment to tell me she had stage four cancer. Until today it amazes me how cut off I was from my father, even if I used to be his favorite child, his first born, who went abroad, went to college, had degrees. But I also never married, came out as a lesbian, exposed secrets about violence in the family and sexual abuse by uncles instead of burying it in shame.

My father suffered delusional paranoia, for a long time evident only in his occasional rambling displeasure about a relative, a minister at the church he ceased to attend. His delusions shot up like weeds after mother passed away, tendrils of fear and rage snaking into every conversation, sparing no one, his children, grandchildren, and neighbors. He grew more and more convinced that his house, the piece of land under his roof was being stolen from him. Physically ill as he was, he refused to live with anyone and refused to have anyone live with him, walled in, withering.

Years after my father's death in 2006, the small piece of land under my father's roof that had always been synonymous for me with *back home* began dislodging from the sweet potato-shaped peninsula flanked by the South China Sea and the Strait of Malacca. Home where walls echoed rage and the thudding sounds of feet, children running from the inescapable fists and cane, pleading, *please appa¹, appa please, won't do it again appa* – where tears soaked pillows rank from sweaty nights and afternoon naps, where rituals of prayer and violence co-existed with grand birthdays and elaborate Christmas *phalahaaram.*² Malaysia quietly slid into the earth, like a slowed motion computerized image of islands being swallowed by the rising seas. No more collapsed identities, no more strained loyalties, no more questioning glances – *You're staying in a hotel? Aren't your parents living here?*

Going home was always complicated regardless of whether I was twenty-one, popping in to see my parents for the weekend from the house I rented eight miles away, or fifty, flying across oceans from America. The fluttering anticipation of being welcomed and being missed mingled and soured with bracing for my father's interrogations – *how much are they paying – how much is your rent – why don't you get a job here –* his guilt trips – *who knows if I'll still be here when you come next time – who knows if you'll get married before I die.*

My mother's way of marking my returns was to cook my favorite fried *kembong*³ fish and *rasam*⁴, the *pandan*⁵-flavored crêpe rolls bursting with grated coconut and dark palm sugar, chocolate cake the color of midnight and light as clouds. My father's way of noting my quick returns was usually a cursory, "Oh you came back," framed as a question. As more years passed between my visits, my mother built the momentum, asking him to buy the ingredients for her baking, reminding him that I was coming, and in the process, I suppose, infecting him with her sense of excitement so that I came home not only to her feasts but to his abundant

---

1 Tamil term for father.

2 Festive savory and sweet foods.

3 Small mackerel.

4 A spicy clear soup made with different ingredients. My mother's *rasam* was tamarind based with sautéed whole black pepper, coriander seed, cumin seed, mustard seed, dried red peppers, and garlic crushed with skin on.

5 Highly aromatic leaf. Also known as screw pine.

fruit purchases—papaya, pineapple, and star fruit that he would peel, slice and serve, and then with a mischievous smile, place small plastic packets of vinegary pickled bright yellow mango slices he had sneaked in during his fruit-buying spree, the contraband junk food he and I would indulge in despite my mother's complaints about vinegar being bad for our health. I enjoyed these moments of celebratory gorging as much as I resented his need to monopolize my time, concocting excuses to avoid being with him, sneaking visits with mum at my sister's home and she having to lie and him finding out anyway and going on jealous tirades. Years later in therapy I would hear and dismiss the therapist's suggestion, "Perhaps he admired your independence but didn't know how to express himself." A Jaffna daughter's independence was an asset if she first carried out her filial duty, which I rejected like a coat of thorns.

A few days after my mother's death, without knowing why, I found myself unscrewing a jar of turmeric powder to inhale the rich aroma. Instantly, it transported me thousands of miles and years to a forgotten scent from when I was a child. My mother would rub crushed turmeric root on her face to soften and cleanse the skin, leaving a sharp raw distinct smell and yellow stains on her fingertips and the blouse she wore for mask days. The deep yellowish orange powder in my kitchen took me back to the scented trail my mother carried through the hallway, from living room to kitchen, as she moved about the house. I had cooked with turmeric for decades. It is a standard spice for any South Asian home, sprinkled over carrots and potatoes, flavoring lentils, complementing the garlic in green squash and coconut milk, boiled in rice with cardamom, the regular must for fish curries. I had no special relationship with the spice, never associated it with my mother until I pressed my nose into the jar.

I remember now that my mother stopped using the turmeric because my father didn't want *his wife's face to look yellowish in public*. I remembered my mother's annoyance. My father had said it was something that Jaffna women did not do. My mother, however, was Indian – her relatives migrated to Malaysia (then called Malaya) from South India. My father was Sri Lankan Tamil, his parents migrated from Jaffna during British colonial rule, when the British were "recruiting"[6] labor to Malaya – for civil service sectors, plantations, tin mines. Jaffna was primarily settled by Tamils of Sri Lanka (then called Ceylon). Apparently when my paternal grandfather walked off the ship bringing Britain's labor force from India and Ceylon to Malaya, he replied in English when asked his name by the officers corralling arrivals. He worked for the post office until he retired.

Dad's death did not immediately open the guarded, barricaded borders between us, and did not free up memories waiting to be found. Unlike stories of my mother, the voice in my head when I recall my father is a jagged monotone, my portrayal of him flat and compressed. There is no fill light for my character portrayals of him, no softer memories to make him interesting. I don't want, and cannot afford, to forget his violence and the impact it left on my siblings, on me, on my mother. He stands in for the father I could not have, a disappointment I carry, a lack for which I grieve.

Funnily, even ironically, the closest I have come to discovering more sides to him is from the dog stories that run through my family history. Dogs were very much a part of our lives. The dog tales surface like photographs, watery outlines seen through the film-processing chemicals in a darkroom, then details filling in quickly, snapshots firing in my brain. These stories have given me the space to connect with my father at another level, as if seeing him from a distance, through a window, a crack between the doors, glimpses of the man he also was.

6 Recruitment included indentured servitude. I speculate that since my paternal grandfather wasn't from a financially privileged class, his English language mission school education while in Jaffna probably spared him being indentured.

There's the story about Jacky, the one master dog. Father brought Jacky home by car. The dog's low growl continuously reverberated across his taut tan torso, ears pressed flat against his head, teeth barring between the tight straps of the muzzle. Jacky had belonged to an old expatriate who worked for Sime Darby and was returning to England on retirement. "He's loyal. Great watch dog. But you have to break him," the Britisher warned as he handed the leash to my father, who like many others had responded to an advertisement. The others were put off— too fierce, they said. But not my father.

I must have been nine or ten, peeking through the crack between the two panel doors leading to the back of the house. My father held a wooden stool in one hand like a lion tamer, a thick stick in the other hand, around which he had wrapped a towel. Jacky's muzzle was off. I heard the dog snarling and holding his ground as my father advanced, yelling, "Sit! Jacky, sit!" When he didn't obey, my father advanced, then hit him. Jacky sprang forward, growling, the stool separating him and my father. The battle between them went on for hours. I felt sad for Jacky. And scared for my father. For two days, Jacky had no food. My father managed to get him into a wooden kennel he had built. As my mother prepared dinner and we chattered around the kitchen, Jacky stayed quiet, the kennel his prison and our protection. My father continued to work on him each day after work, rewarding him with food when he obeyed, yelling down snarls and growls when Jacky resisted. My mother was convinced we had to call the SPCA and send the dog away. My father persisted. Gradually, the growls and snaps and snarls eased. Between the stick, the stool, and alternating between giving him food and denying it, my father prevailed. Jacky did break. But he reserved his devotion for my father. To the rest of the family, he was a ferocious mean dog, a terror to all the other dogs that passed the house, the neighbors, the postman, the garbage collectors. My siblings and I could not walk him. We were afraid to get too close to his kennel. Only my father was allowed to interact with him. Eventually, my father was able to brush and bathe him. And even play tug-of-war with a rag toy made of old bed sheet strips tied up in a bunch.

The Britisher had given my father a food list for Jacky. Sausages. Raw red meat to nurture his fierceness. Boiled beef bones to gnaw on and strengthen his teeth. My father fed Jacky curry and rice, boiled pig skin and vegetables for soup so the fat would bring gloss to his hair, rewarding him with dog biscuits when he did what he was told. He talked to Jacky in Tamil and English, his accented commands slowly taking over the sound of the previous master's voice.

Years later, when my father had his first stroke and was in the hospital for at least two weeks, Jacky refused to eat. By then Jacky was accustomed to the rest of the family and we could walk him although we still dared not touch him. When we told my father that Jacky was not eating, he insisted on coming home early from the hospital against my mother's wishes. The day he came home, Jacky leapt up after not moving for days, wagging his tail at the sound of my father's voice, the mean one-master dog suddenly turning into a weak, happy puppy. I think having to nurse Jacky back to health made my father stronger faster. And having my father back made Jacky a little less scary. He never did become a house pet like our other dogs that came and went from our family, but Jacky did become more at home.

My second dog memory is framed by a flash flood in the early 1970s that took over the capital and outlying areas. Two rivers in Kuala Lumpur overflowed like never before and flooded the city and its surrounding districts. Water climbed up the walls. Buses, cars, houses were submerged. The mosque at the bottom of the hill where we lived seemed to float, water halting halfway up the green tiled dome. My family had moved a year before and we lived up a hill, cut off from everything below, watching men in boats rowing down a sea of brown water over what used to be roads. My grandmother's house was further away. They had been evacuated quickly. When she and Aunty Esther bundled their clothes, locked the house, and got into Uncle Joseph's car, they forgot Puppy. He was their big dog, all black, and barking nonstop at everything that passed the house. I thought he was the Hound of the Baskervilles. My father said that Puppy needed a bigger cage and more exercise. Aunty Esther took him out in the morning and night so he could stretch his legs and empty his bowels. Otherwise, he sat hunched over in the cage, his ears pointed straight up, his snout pressed against the metal bars.

No one thought the flood would last long. We'd never had a flood before. But the waters stayed up to my father's thighs even after five days. Aunty Esther telephoned from a cousin's house and said Puppy was still at home. My father took the news as if someone in our family had been run over by a car. He was shocked, and kept saying to my mother, "How could they just leave the dog?" He was ready to wade over to my grandmother's house, rescue Puppy, maybe imagining the worst but saying nothing to us. The news over the transistor radio warned people not to venture out. There was a health advisory about dead pigs and chickens floating in the water. A neighbor said that the flood had released several crocodiles from a crocodile farm; mother panicked, insisting against my father going out because of a dog. Father got agitated. He was obsessed by the fact that Puppy was abandoned.

Two days later, when the water receded to his calves, my father and a friend ventured out, rolling up their trousers, carrying their slippers to keep from losing them. They managed to get into the house where the water had subsided even further. My father later told my mother that the cardboard walls that separated the bedrooms in my grandmother's house had buckled, and thick orange silt blanketed everything. At the back of the house he found Puppy trapped in his cage, so bloated they couldn't get him out. My father had to leave him. He went back later with friends, a claw hammer and *parang*[7] to break open the door of the cage. He returned late that day, washed, ate, and didn't talk to anyone. Then he and mum stayed locked in my parent's room for hours. I even thought I heard him crying.

We stopped calling Puppy a crazy dog after that. He became Poor Puppy who drowned in the flood. Or Poor Puppy who dad tried to save even though he had drowned long before my father got to him.

Perhaps reliving the dog tales are a way to negotiate my exile from my father and help me return him to my siblings, to me. Perhaps recalling the dog tales will help me feel compassion for the man he was, without letting him off the hook for the terrifying, bullying ways he ruled our home. These stories are a way of tracing my father's life through different memories. It is like giving his grave a specially commissioned family headstone, white marble instead of the plain stone marker we settled on from the funeral home. Perhaps it is the only way I can be dutiful to a man who wanted me to be his badge of honor and glory, his pride to show off to friends and relatives, the daughter in America.

---

7 A kind of machete.

OFF THE BODY

Janet Jones

1.

Changing landscapes of body reshape territorial markers of my
    exile,
Made new and savagely familiar day by day.
Threads of fractured mind
Where joy holds on against stacked odds,
And enjoys the peace of my own acceptance.
Reaching a summary in motion,
Criss-crossed intersections reveal themselves,
A myriad of starting points.

2.

Burst through rape seed yellow, just go, just go.
I have a tribe, exiled rails into the unknown.
Shared intimacy, and alone, together,
Desire and isolation, some comfort.
Exile is a place we dwell,
A landscape,
A territory, bigger than an imposition.

Homophobic edge, wasn't it?
We shared a taste in women and that cut through.
For a moment, experiential place meant more than my
    gender politics,
How can that work?
Port in a storm priority won out,
Not for long, but long enough.

3.

"So what's different about a butch in a wheelchair?" You say,
"I know plenty of femmes who do manual trades."
In my mind I'm picking you up right around your waist,
Half putting, half throwing you on the bed,
A few moments slide and my fingers are inside you.
"Well, femmes could do that too," I hear you say.
I know but I'm butch, it's not the same.
I feel the attitude, the approach and it's different,
It's just different.

4.

Different codes, changing language of what you see in me, and
     how I see myself,
Semiotic wilderness.

5.

Changing body exiles me from physical territory that was once
     my own,
With no watch towers or angry dogs.
A betrayal of sorts, from within, the new exile from whom I was.
Grief and loss, the perennial wanderers of the world.

6.

Not able to function in the world with pressure from a
     challenged mind,
I find it hard to reach for lesbian hands.

7.

You didn't order me out, but I don't fit.

8.

Not free to name the homophobic onslaught
That took my childhood mind,

I'm lost in circles in woods with no map
No skills to read signs or find a way back.
Razor wire and dogs,
The bad publicity of lesbian mental health,
Stops me reaching for your hand
Anyway I didn't learn how
While my feet trip me later.

9.
A world lacking
The imagination or skill
To bring us in,
We work on parallel creations.

10.
I can't do lesbian sex, fashion or politics anymore,
Retreating along fibers and bones.
If I had just made it through enough
Lesbian intersectionalities
Maybe I wouldn't have been exiled.

Photo Credit: Natasa Velikonja

The Refusal of Exile: Ljubljana Lesbians Standing Their Ground the Morning After Their Gathering Place Was Firebombed," 2010. This image was used as the book cover for *Vecno Vojo Stanje* (Eternal State of War) by Urška Sterle, Slovenian lesbian activist. The words on the wall call for "death to all queers." Image used with permission of the photographer and author.

MY LIFE ON A PAGE

Dovey Dee

*B*eing *born in southern Louisiana and raised in southern California has provided me with a particular insight into America's cultural schizophrenia: highly creative and innovative and yet at times superficial; genteel and racist; iconoclastic and bound by tradition. I migrated to Australia in 2000. This move was a voluntary, but daunting dislocation. In some ways, marked by exile. While Australian immigration recognizes samesex de facto partnerships, American does not. Furthermore, neither country recognizes same-sex marriage. Had that not been the case at the time of my immigration to Australia, my partner and I would have had the freedom to move between countries unencumbered, without the finality of the decision to leave one country for the other. The enormity of this move took its toll on my body.*

But mingled with my ever-present homesickness is the wonder and excitement of discovering my adopted homeland. The light of the southern hemisphere is cast from the north and the sun literally bites the skin. We depend on sunlight and landscape to orient ourselves and I literally lost direction for a while. But the Australian landscape is like no other and is a challenging subject for an artist. I now understand the awe and inspiration of living in a totally strange land and trying to capture it in paint. Living here has changed me, changed my art, and literally changed my heart.

I have grown to understand and love Aboriginal indigenous art. It is truly all about their land and their dreamtime and is painted from a visual perspective that is unknown to the Eurocentric mode of "seeing." The tragedy of First Australians is that they are nearly exiles in their own country, but they have their collective vision as a guidepost to their enduring culture.

I am a stranger in this land, but I have learned to see it with my heart and my memory. I do not paint or see as an indigenous

Australian—I cannot possibly—but I have adapted to the harsh southern sunlight, the grey-greens of the eucalypt forests and the brick red, iron ore soil. It is indeed a land of little rain. You drink when you can, and when you do have water for your soul, it is sweet.

I wrote this short essay, "My Life on a Page," in February 2012 to accompany an exhibition of my landscape paintings that were displayed in a group show at the Louis Joel Gallery in Altona, Victoria, Australia. The exhibition, called "Life and Stories," was part of the gay and lesbian annual celebration of LGBT culture in Victoria called "Midsumma." The focus of the group exhibition was personal stories, perspectives, and viewpoints of gay and lesbian artists and writers. All the artists were asked to write a short essay about their personal lives. I chose to write an open love letter to my dearest partner, Libby.

January 27, 2012

My Dearest Libby,

You have gotten me into so much trouble. In these past eighteen years, my life with you has been a challenge, a joy, a heartache, a raucous laugh, and an adventure. How can I describe my naiveté about things to come that day when we met in Long Beach, California? Me: pale and morose from living in upstate New York and recovering from a calamitous and bitter break up with my long-term partner. You: cheerful, bright, sunny and exotic. Oh, yes, also separated from your husband, caring for your two adolescent boys, and planning to return to Australia as soon as you were able. I was smitten; what could possibly go wrong?

I had made a conscious choice in my life not to have children. Not just because I was gay, but rather was raised at a time when having children meant loss of life choices, and career choices were limited enough for women. I struggled hard to have a real career, both as an artist and as a computer scientist and engineer. My work had me exhibiting in art galleries and museums around greater Los Angeles and contributing to engineering projects that bought me into association with some of the highest levels of environmental management in the U.S. Department of Defense. You admitted that your work was your children: making sure that they were happy, healthy, safe and had the chance to experience the richness of life. You said the one thing to me that would make me adore you forever: "My children will always come first."

So I found myself in the new, exciting, odd, and sometimes uncomfortable role of being the proxy responsible adult in the lives of two young boys. It was so hard for them. It was terrifying for me. Thankfully I had your constant optimism to rely upon. There was so much uncertainty to which all of us had to adjust. We all muddled through, learned to adapt, and to care for each other despite our frailties. And I learned more about myself than I could have possibly imagined. Now we are on the brink of grandparenthood and I am grateful for the chance to see you hold your little bundle of hereditary genetics.

Until I met you, living in Australia was never on my radar —not even visiting Australia. Yet in 1998 you declared that you would return to Melbourne in 2000, and I could come along or not. You offered the same choice to your sons. Let's see: selling everything I own, leaving my job, leaving my family and friends, packing up my dog, and moving to a continent that I had only visited twice, with you. What could possibly go wrong? I was thrilled and petrified when we moved to Melbourne in January 2000. As your de facto partner, I was given permanent residency status immediately. I remember thinking how civilized that was, that Australia was so much more advanced than the U.S. concerning samesex relationships.

The immediate access to health care proved to be indescribably fortunate that horrific day shortly after we moved to Melbourne. The terrible chest pains, the sweating, the call to emergency services, the poor puzzled dog that had to be put outdoors while I waited for the ambulance to arrive. I managed to call you at work and as the paramedics loaded me into the ambulance, you arrived home in time to ride with me to the hospital. Somewhere around Yarraville I actually died in the ambulance. You were very scared and distraught as you sat and watched the paramedics electrocute me back to life. And as I recovered consciousness, it was your lovely face, your hands cradling my head, and your voice telling me that it would all be okay that filled my awareness. I was destined to be yours for years to come and not to die in a 7-Eleven parking lot on Somerville Road.

Going on nineteen years, we continue on this journey together, literally reborn in a new country, and I cannot imagine doing this with anyone but you. Thank you, darlin'. At times we may have been a trial for each other, but we have never been bored. You still make me laugh until I choke with tears. You have fulfilled all of the requirements and wishes that I have ever wanted for a partner in my life: a true helpmate, a marvellous dancer, a searing wit, and a girl from the South. I just didn't know how far South I would end up having to go.

IT'S WHY I WORE RED

Voltrina Williams

The air is stifling as I walk past your casket. The Bethel Missionary Baptist Church probably had never felt such an intense heat. Hell couldn't wait to get you, so it just crawled up out of the hot, red Georgia clay to claim you early, it seems.

My best friend warned me not to come.

"Why even pretend to mourn the loss of such a vile person?" she asked me.

But knowing me better than anyone else, you know full well that I had to see you dead with my own eyes.

Daddy, you are the man to whom I owe my very existence . . . but more so, my distinct lack thereof an existence. Now your body lies as stiff as your dick that you forced in me, time and time again. See Daddy, we both know that I was your hidden child—the one the newspaper headlines, the folks at your job, the folks at your home church, and just about everyone else who really mattered didn't even know about. I'm your dirty, love-child-secret— the one who your wife (who sits there crying after seventy years of married "bliss") had to forgive. Yeah, this love child has secrets all right. Secrets that I kept for you until your dying day.

Why?

You know damn well why. It was because you were all I had, and we both know that you took full advantage of that.

It wasn't until after the aneurism took Mama that you first penetrated me; but I realize now, that I had been being groomed all along. The ice cream parties on the patio, the expensive dresses, the makeup when I was way too young . . . all of that made me your princess-mistress too. I wonder if your hands are any colder now than when they touched me the very first time. I don't remember because I was only four. Yes, it's hot as hell in here, Daddy, but not as hot as where you've gone.

You made sure that you were the one that comforted me, an "orphaned child" with nowhere else to go. You and your wife were "saints" for taking me in. At least that's what they all said. To the world, I was your niece. To your wife, I was the object of her most vile resentment. See, every time you upset her, I got to suffer your punishment. She was too weak to stand up to you, but standing up on my back was never a problem for her. I was the dilemma . . . the predicament . . . the situation. Everyone did get privy to know when my grade wasn't high enough, or I said the wrong thing, dated the wrong one, or didn't fit the impossibly perfect mold she created to shove me into.

You would have thought running away would have solved my problem. Yeah, I did too. You could have washed your hands of me and written me off to the streets I had turned to. But you didn't. Rather, to extend my torture, you disguised your deceit as love. The apartment you bought for me wasn't "free." It never was intended to be free. I paid for it just about every time you could steal a moment away from your wife.

"Oh, he is spending the evening with his wayward daughter/niece? How admirable!"

None of them knew that I saw more of your cock than your wife ever did. I didn't tell because I was in survival mode and you knew it . . . you designed it. You made sure I knew enough about the world to know that the cold slap of the streets was worse than the slap on my behind that got you off. Eating your ass was better than being hungry. After all, I have a master's degree, a paid for home, a decent car, and a hatred towards men to show for it. What a deal, Daddy!

Hell, no, I don't want to sit with "the family." What role do I pretend to fit into? Daughter, niece, lover, mistress, wife—fuck it all. Let them cry the real tears. They don't even know you. They don't know that it was me that got the realest you of all. Stepma doesn't even know you smoke Black & Milds after you eat pussy. Thanks for both of those habits too, Dad.

You know, I did sit through half your service. Then the bullshit and lies started to really make my head hurt. Yeah, everyone is so damn great after they are dead. Everyone gets selective amnesia of all of the shit the person did while they were living, and you're lucky for that. You're also lucky that I'm not drunk enough or brave enough to march right up into the pulpit and tell it all. I wonder why no one asked me to make any remarks.

No, Daddy, I will keep our secrets. The things you left to me in the will were generous, but they were only for show. You took care of me quite well before the will was even written and I kept that as a secret too. I take from you my lessons that I learned the hard way. Let's see . . . I learned how to be the best paid whore around. I learned that my worth is between my legs and how fast I can shake my hips. I learned that love is unconditional as long as I swallowed. I learned men are never to be trusted, especially when they are kind. Yes, thanks, Daddy, for everything you taught me. Now you can rest peacefully in hell.

I did hear the gasps from your sisters as I grabbed the tail of my dress when I headed out the door. I'm sure they will talk for months about the ungrateful hussy who wore red.

HERE,
WHERE EVEN THE ROCKS HAVE NAMES

Terry Martin

Having traveled decades together,
the two are putting down roots,
here, where even the rocks have names.
Sagebrush and thistle mark craggy hills,
ground squirrels scrabble the dust.

Rising off the open field,
a circling hawk rides its thermal
conserving its energy for other things.

Earlier this year, their neighbor
cut away acres of trees.
Gala apples no longer exist.
Planted in their place,
flimsy vines of wine grapes
in long straight rows.
In time, Syrah will be bottled,
will improve with age.

Listening to trills from distant birds
they cannot name, the two try to imagine
ways they will take this place into them,
how it may shape what they will become.

YAKIMA POSTCARD, TO CAREL

Terry Martin

Now it's July, abundantly.
All over the valley, cherry trees are letting go.
Branches hang low, weighted with ripeness.
Boughs bending, bending—
a kind of forgiveness curving toward us.

We're thinking of you in Olympia,
caring round-the-clock for Lynn
through this last, hardest part.
Doing all it takes
so the one you love most
can be home, with you,
where she belongs.
Giving your all,
the way a fruit tree empties itself,
then fills again, and again.

Here, mourning doves coo.
We stumble along rutted lanes of grass,
gleaning Bings, Rainiers, pie cherries, too.
Gathering what we can hold.

WHILE YOU'RE IN D.C.

Terry Martin

I think about the three-hour time difference.
I think about your meeting with the senator.
I think about Kramer's Bookstore and Coffee Shop,
in DuPont Circle, their motto that we love:
If we had a shower, you could live here.

I think about what I forgot to tell you
on the phone yesterday—Helen's confused
and confusing call from Assisted Living,
the "yes" letter I got from *Calyx*,
two pheasants preening in the cherry orchard,
the first iris blooming.
Our dog—ears flat, tail tucked—
moping and sighing while you're away.

I think about where you are, the poetry of that city,
imagine us there together, walking
arm in arm down a cobblestone street,
like a river under the stars.

Home, surrounded by things that remind me of you
(a basket, a sweatshirt, a candle, a bowl)
I think about how different you and I are.
Like square differs from round, round from square.
How it's been twenty-five years
of unbroken conversation across a scarred table.
How you see the me I can't bear to.

I want to know, a country apart,
same sun shining above both our heads,
what bracelets circle your wrist today
what your hand is reaching for
whether you hear church bells ringing.

Photo Credit: Khaela Maricich

Jeanine Oleson, *The Greater New York Smudge Cleanse*, public performance on November 3, 2008, shown: event at Federal Hall, Lower Manhattan

A public art project applying the ancient practice of smoking out dormant bad energies to contemporary challenges including environmental pollution in Greenpoint and Gowanus Canal, Brooklyn; gentrification driving queer communities out of Manhattan's West Village; and pre-election anxiety/U.S. economic imperialism on the steps of Federal Hall with dancers and a tarot reader.

Jeanine Oleson, Magic on Women's Mountain, 2009, Solar
plate etching of Arches, 20 x 24 inches.

LIFEBOAT

Lara Fergus

A utopic tragedy in several panicked voices

– So what do we do now?
– I don't know. Row, I suppose. Everyone got an oar?
– Ouf! This is going to take a while. Can we try and get a rhythm going?
– Why aren't you rowing?
– I'm thinking.
– Can't you think and row at the same time?
– Not properly.
– Do we know which way we're supposed to be rowing?
– Not really—let's sort it out. Who's got a compass?
– A compass! We're not falling into that old "technology will save us" routine already are we?
– OK. We'll go by the stars then.
– Right. Which direction do we row until it gets dark?
– Until we know where we're actually going it doesn't really matter does it?
– Stop being so defeatist.
– I'm not being defeatist. I was just stating a point.
– Sarcastically.
– What are you, the tone police?
– I think the situation is stressful enough without us getting negative.
– What's stressful about it? It couldn't be any better. This is exactly what we wanted.
– I don't know. I sort of miss the Big Ship.
– What! How can you miss it? It was horrible.
– All those inane people by the pool, so full of themselves.
– Being served cocktails, don't forget. Being waited on hand and bloody foot. I mean the exploitation!

- But I miss the cocktails.
- I couldn't afford them. But I liked the idea of them.
- How can you say that? I mean "cocktails"? Even the name.
- The cinema, then. Don't you miss that a bit?
- Mind-numbing propaganda.
- I don't miss the Big Ship at all. I don't miss anything about it. I hope I never see it again.
- Me neither. I was so happy to finally jump ship.
- See I didn't jump—I was pushed.
- Well, we were all pushed, more or less. I jumped at the last minute.
- Just keep rowing would you—you're slowing us down.
- But where? Where?!
- She's right—we've got to sort out where we're going.
- Did anyone bring any fresh water?
- I mean, we need direction. To have one.
- And to row towards it together. All of us. In a synchronized fashion.
- Hang on, that's real Big Ship thinking that. I don't think we need to be synchronized. We can just row.
- Or we can just sit here. Or we can just lie back and stare at the scorching sun as we waste away and are wiped from memory . . .
- You think we'll be forgotten? You think this will come to nothing?
- Maybe we should have stayed on the Big Ship. We could have mutinied, taken control by force. Then we could have gone wherever we wanted much quicker.
- Oh, come on. Nice idea, but what about all those people who don't want to go where we want to go?
- Well, then we take control by ideas. We educate them, we gradually occupy positions of power until one day—Captain! Then we can set the course we want.

- Are you kidding? It would take ages, and even if you eventually got a hold of the wheel, do you have any idea how long it takes to turn one of those things around?
- Whereas with something small like this you can do really tight circles—look.
- Would you stop it! I feel sick enough as it is.
- Me too. I think I'll go back.
- What are you talking about? You can't go back—it's miles away by now.
- No, it must just be over the horizon—we're still attached to it.
- What?!
- We're still attached—look at these ropes just under the water.
- Oh, my god, she's right. What do we do?
- Cut them—who's got a knife?
- First I'd like to confirm that someone has fresh water.
- Forget the water. Who's got a knife?
- But what if there's no land? What if there are no other ships? What if the Big Ship's all there is?
- Pull yourself together, woman! Of course we'll find land.
- What if it's already inhabited? I don't like where this is going.
- Me neither. Help pull me in—I want to go back.
- No way—we've got to cut these ropes.
- I've got family on the Big Ship.
- We've all got family on the Big Ship.
- I wonder if they've noticed we're gone?
- Not mine. I made a clone of myself before I left. Looks like me, sounds like me, but only talks about the weather.
- You made a clone! How on earth can you justify that?
- To stop people getting hurt!
- Let her go back then. If she doesn't want to be here, she clearly doesn't belong here.

- Oh, so it's you who decides who belongs here and who doesn't, is it?
- She said she didn't want to be here!
- I said I wanted to go back! I didn't say permanently.
- Well if you're not a hundred percent committed to the lifeboat, I don't see what your interest is in it at all.
- It's all or nothing, is it?
- No—just that you're either with us or against . . .
- Oh! You know who you sound like!
- This is different.
- Why?
- It's a matter of intention. It's a matter of context.
- Everything's relative?
- How dare you!
- Hang on, wait. Let's think about this. Maybe it's better that we stay attached just while we're sorting out what to do. I mean we've got no water and we don't know where we're going.
- I know where we're going. I just don't know how to get there.
- If we had some tools from the Big Ship we could work out a course.
- Would you stop this childish reliance on the Big Ship! We can work it out without them.
- But we might get there quicker with some of their stuff.
- Not while we're being dragged along! I can't believe we're even considering staying attached.
- You know what? I don't think a lifeboat's really what we want.
- What are you talking about? It's not a matter of what we want, it's a matter of what we don't want.
- I don't want the Big Ship.
- I don't want to die! Where's the water?
- What we don't want is hierarchy. We don't want any one group dominating any other group. Did you see the way

those cabins are organized on the Big Ship? And the slave holds below?

– No cabins here.

– No.

– You know what we should have got? A tug boat.

– What?

– Not a lifeboat, a tug boat.

– Oh, boring! Who wants to spend their life trying to pull some heavy thing around?

– Well, I don't want to spend my life in a four-meter-squared prison, exposed to the elements.

– But in order to tug them you've got to get them to cut the engine, and how are you going to achieve that?

– I read that there isn't an engine—we've just been led to believe there is.

– Oh, there's an engine. And we'd need an engine powerful enough to pull them. This is worse than the mutiny idea.

– Well, excuse me for trying. But you'll admit this isn't ideal?

– What isn't?

– This lifeboat! Out here in the middle of nowhere. Being pulled along.

– You're right. That's why we've got to cut the ropes.

– But in that case we either drift, or we decide on a direction and we row towards it.

– Right.

– But what are we rowing towards? I mean, is it an island, a land mass, another Big Ship? Will there be other people?

– I don't know.

– No, no other people—at least we're not going to colonize anyone.

– And I suppose we're not going to get colonized.

– Not again, no way! We'll be on the look out this time.

– So no other people.

– Well, that's OK isn't it? We get along, don't we?

SHIFTING TERRITORIES

Yael Mishali

To Ilay

1.

A daydream: A woman is cooking on a steamy afternoon. Her armpits are moist and her cheeks are rosy. A Mizrahi song is playing in the background; the floor is wet like her body and the amount of light is precise, like spice. Her face is my mother's face, and I can almost hear one of my brothers crying in his crib in the next room, but you come from behind, hug me, strong like the man my mother always wanted behind; and in front of me the food reaches a boiling point and I am bubbling and you do not let me cool off. I am fixing you a plate of desire, but we eat alongside the pot, standing up, steam streams besides our bodies. You take me and bring me back, reminding me that it's me, under this floral apron.

Mizrahi and Ashkenazi are categories of ethnicity that serve to classify the Jewish-Israeli population into two distinct groups. Mizrahi refers to Jews who immigrated to Israel mainly from Arab and Muslim countries while Ashkenazi refers to Jews who immigrated to Israel from western European countries as well as English-speaking countries in the Americas. Like black and white, Mizrahi and Ashkenazi are cultural categories that hold class and economic value, as well as both positive and negative symbolic meaning.

"*Ata Chayav Lamut Alay*" (You Must Love Me) was the first Mizrahi song I listened to on my own, initially the Hebrew version and later in Moroccan. Before this moment, I have never chosen to listen to Mizrahi music out of my own free will. Like many of my friends, whose ethnic origins were deemed irrelevant, I believed Mizrahi music was too weepy, or something to laugh about. The first time I let myself listen to a Mizrahi song repeatedly was while I was working on a drag show. On stage I was as Moroccan as I could be, in dress, movement and voice way before I was ready to be so in real life. Through a song that presents a Mizrahi woman of whom it is clear that there is no man who can resist her I wanted to make a double passing—from someone who looks like a straight Ashkenazi woman to the Mizrahi femme I am, who by perfectly imitating the language of the women who preceded her, entices imagined butches. Only after the performance, when there was no longer a reason to memorize the song and I still heard it playing in my head, could I admit that it aroused in me what I thought I had willingly hidden.

My mother always wanted us to get our hair straightened. Ever since I can remember, she saved newspaper clippings that reported the latest updates from the hair stylists on how to control unruly hair. Ever since I was a little girl, my mother, fascinated by the beauty of women with straight hair, would tell me our hair was a calamity and spend hours blow drying her hair straight. When I came out of the closet at the age of sixteen, I cut my hair short, intertwining ethnic and sexual stereotypes—lesbians have short hair and Moroccans have hair like steel wool. In 2003 I wore my hair down for the first time, femmeness was the first context to allow it.

Growing up I learned that not only didn't the Moroccan accent and pronunciation sound smart, they are even considered linguistic errors, and I started listening to my mother through a permanent filter—silently correcting her, lest her "mistakes" be ingrained in me. Outside the house I heard many words that I didn't completely understand, but I knew exactly how to say them. Eventually I succeeded in passing—an Ashkenazi name was written on all letters addressed to me—Mishali was given a new spelling, without the guttural "*ayin.*"

I started thinking about myself as a lesbian at sixteen after telling another girl from school that I love volunteering at self-defense classes but when the instructor is on top of me and I am supposed to push her away I blush and freeze and she said casually, "It sounds normal to me, but I am a lesbian." That word, which resonated something vague in me that as a child in a conservative Moroccan family I had heard before only in late-night-strange-scary movies, made me feel for the first time that there was a word for what I was. Since that moment I went out, slept and fell in love with women, but always continued to feel like an outsider, the same way I felt before around straight girls. I never felt qualified to be a lesbian, and knew that since I don't look like one my status could be easily revoked.

As a Moroccan Arab Jew, I always felt on both sides—black in my eyes and white in my skin, Mizrahi at home and Ashkenazi outside of it. Born and raised to hate my heritage while rewriting my history in a foreign language, trying to cross the borders, I discovered all barriers reside in me. Never looking back or sounding the way I am supposed to, I have grown accustomed to living on the border, hesitant to choose sides, knowing that a part of me won't survive the transition. In this occupied territory, I could only be the shifting component —the ally and the enemy, the daughter of the oppressor and of the oppressed, fighting for some names while others are being forced on me, struggling to stay because I have nowhere else to go.

2.

There is yet another closet for me to come out of, but nothing is waiting for me on the other side, not even a language. If a lesbian coming out story is primarily based on a binary metaphor in which one is moving from slavery (men) to freedom (women)—how can I ever come out? What aspects of me will become silenced when I will allegedly say everything I have to say about myself?

A short while ago we went to see the Hebrew version of the lesbian play "Last Summer at Bluefish Cove" which was produced by the local gay theater company and hosted in the Tel Aviv gay community center. I was moved not only as a lesbian, but also as a woman who does not completely obey the anorectic decree of womanhood since the role of the most desirable woman, the one they were all fantasizing about, was played by a vivacious woman with a body similar to my own. I felt represented at the most intimate level—that my body, my desires and my thoughts are relevant, exciting and sexy, and even important enough to be in a play. But whenever I got emotional during the performance and squeezed my partner's hand, I could imagine the women in the audience looking at us, sneering and thinking, "Who are those straighties who came to watch a show about lesbians?"

You can call our love story a transgendered story, not just because it began years earlier and in another gender time. Although we became a couple only after he had already started his transition, we went through most of it together, and even today he actively includes his gender past in our relationship as well as in his personal life in general. As someone who used to be mainly with butch people, some of whom even passed as men, it took me a while to note any change. At first he received a lot of the same questioning reactions as my exes used to get. Then slowly I began to notice that the same look that used to mark me indirectly as a lesbian, this time conveyed a new and unfamiliar kind of reservation, but I was still happy that we weren't viewed as a normal couple. But after two years and unmistakably after five, he passed regularly. And from the moment he passed as a man, I automatically started passing as straight and we both lost our queer identities.

As a lesbian who is in love with a transman, how can I explain my position without disavowing his? Is the only way to protect his name to give up mine?

When we attend big LGBT events we are often asked if we are straight. My partner answers, "No, I am trans and she is femme." This was more than once followed by, "Oh, so you are dykes." Is there a way for me to keep being a lesbian without dragging him along, thereby confirming the transphobic assumption that underneath it all every transman is a woman? Even people who know us are struggling to understand why it is so important to us what other people think. Most of them can't imagine being at the same time invisible to your own and too visible to the rest. They can't figure out what it means for me to lose the only look in the street which did not read my body as an invitation for harassment, but actually identified in me for a moment, beyond ridicule, dismissal or disgust, an independent desire. They can't picture that glare from someone I used to know who sees us in the street holding hands and whispers in my ear, "Oh, so eventually we lost you as well." Even other couples like us don't always share our pain, and I know of a few women who don't mind being viewed as straight. Even if this is truly fine for some of us, I wonder, how many times we women are expected to give up our names (as much as they are "ours") for a new name devoid of history?

Given that Hebrew is a gendered language, almost every sentence requires a sex determination. When my partner talks about his past, he uses feminine pronouns which can embarrass even queer people around us not to mention threaten transpeople who feel inherently represented by this whether it suits them or not.

When we first arrived to see the apartment we live in today after months of searching, we instantly spotted the rainbow flag hanging from the window and saw it as a sign that this was our new home. A short time after we settled in, we got a call from our landlord demanding that we take down at once "the homo rag" from her building. We knew she felt comfortable saying that to us since she thought we were "a normal couple" and assumed the flag was left hanging by mistake, a coincidental inheritance from the gay couple who had lived there before us. I wanted to yell at her that I have no intention of removing the flag, and that I knew the only reason she made nice with the wealthy, white, Ashkenazi gay men who used to live there was she liked the fact that they had replaced all the lighting fixtures in the apartment at their own expense, but I kept quiet. After ending the call still shocked and disappointed in myself for not answering back, it suddenly dawned on me—what exactly would I have said? That I am keeping the flag because I am a lesbian and my boyfriend is a transman? What would she understand by that and could we have stayed after she realized we were not who she thought we were, and that we didn't even have two huge paychecks to compensate for it? We are not blind to the privileges we get when we pass as straight in everyday life, but whenever a plumber arrives to fix a leak, ignores my questions and asks to talk to my husband, I have trouble breathing and I am not sure this is the life I chose or how different it is from the one planned for me.

In 2009 we went to support West Jerusalem's pride parade, one of the most controversial parades in Israel, and stayed in the city afterwards for a queer celebration. Around midnight we left the party and started walking towards our car. The streets were still packed with amused teenagers sitting around waiting for the perverts to pass by, shouting, "Go home, the parade is over." When we realized that one of us, a transwoman who does not pass, was getting too much attention, we tried to walk faster, but before we knew it we were surrounded by a group of boys. The one to get the first blow was my boyfriend, a trans guy who may pass as gay and I, who jumped to defend his body thinking my "normal" femininity makes me immune to beatings, was second. It obviously started as a transphobic attack but continued as what—a homophobic one? Lesbophobic? Misogynistic? Who was I when I was beaten?

As a girl who has a boyfriend, where is this need to keep a connection to my lesbian identity coming from? Why is it so hard for me to give this name up? Can I identify as a lesbian without being viewed as someone who has betrayed herself, him, or the lesbian community? Can I not identify as lesbian without turning my back on my history or denying my debt to my lesbian mothers without whom I would probably already be another kind of mother and a wife?

In each and every call from my mother I stop breathing for a moment, praying that no one from our extended family had gotten married in the passing week. I know that every wedding story has a fixed routine: what the bride wore, how beautiful and delicate the groom was, and how everything was classy and properly organized. Then it's my turn and she demands, "So, don't you have anything to tell me?" And I, who know that no matter what I have to tell, it's not the story she wants to hear, say, "Mom, stop." Since my boyfriend and I became a couple, I have kept my everyday life under my tongue. But during one call which took place only a week after the shooting in the Tel Aviv gay youth center, I couldn't hold it in any longer. I told her that whoever did this hates people like me, and she replied, "Don't ask me to accept this; I will never be able to see you with another woman." I kept saying, "You don't know anything about my life," until she stopped talking and shouted, "What, what don't I know?" and I took in a few deep breaths and said quickly, "I have a boyfriend, but it's not what you think." And before she had the chance to react I added, "He wasn't born a man." And she asked, "But does he look like a man?" and I said "yes" and she continued, "Ashkenazi?" I confirmed—half ashamed, half proud. And then she presented me with the question I could hear she was holding in. "And can he get you pregnant?" At that point I was already laughing, relieved she wasn't crying or yelling and just said half-jokingly, "By the time I would like to get pregnant it's going to be by artificial insemination anyway, so what does it matter?" Somehow I felt that if I used a term she had heard repeatedly on hyer favourite soaps it would help her think it's a little more normal. She was unusually silent for a moment and I knew that it meant she was yet to completely comprehend what I was saying, and I also knew the word "transgender" wouldn't mean anything to her, so I searched for words she had taught me. I said, "He's a guy, but he has the heart of a girl."

"Fine, whatever, bring him over on Shabbat so we can see him."

When we arrived at Friday's night dinner, everybody was already waiting for us around the table. I went to wash up from the drive and when I returned, I saw my boyfriend sitting next to my brother and father with a yamaka on his head that my mother had given him, just like she does with any of my secular brothers when they come to visit. Today, whenever she calls, she asks about him and invites us to Shabbat dinner. Only one little thing she asks of me. "Sweetheart, my beloved, just don't tell anyone about this. Keep it between us. If anyone asks say straight away he is a regular guy."

every time we step out into the street we are playing a man and a woman but they see a boy and a whore and sometimes they ask us if you are my brother and we both think that if anything you are my sister you stick a cigarette behind your ear to appear more intimidating but we are the only ones who are afraid i wrap around your arm a pain that deepens between my breasts which find cover under a fabric shield we cross the street where there is no room for crossing which is not black and white we cross a street and a ban to love without noticing where we are and how we look trying to overlook how much we are being looked at and you realize you can't look straight into the eyes of every man who penetrates my body with his eyes because your false threat will become his real one to be us in the street is to be where they see me and don't see us where you are worried that they could see you weren't always you and when you go out to buy cigarettes and are asked for your id you laugh and don't think about what they will do if they see the small print because today you are passing and when you come to me on a very hot day starting to undress in the stairwell thankful for the freedom of darkness, I open my door to your chest shining with sweat playfully you push your chest at me shaping breasts with your hands offering your mouth for a kiss asking "how do i look? like a transvestite?" and i hug everything you are and can be and thank god for another day you arrived to me safe and sound.

---

* I thank Debbie Cohen, my chosen sister, for the English edit. I also thank Joan Nestle for giving me a history to belong to beyond geographical boundaries, and for her unique way with words which has continually inspired new ways in me to feel and articulate myself.

BETTER MAN: IT SHOULD'VE BEEN ME
C. Arellano

Twist on old skool song called "It Should Have Been Me" sung by Yvonne Fair.

mother and sister wrestled my ponytail into a bun
they cleopatra'd my eyes
scarlett o'hara'd my lips

down the aisle,
my teen legs stumbled in too-high high heels
drowned in lavender floral chiffon

during the reception,
i told my new sister
what i couldn't tell blood brother in army greens:
i love my best friend

she promised secrecy
next day he called me
if anyone ever bothers you
i got an M16 in my office

i take his oath to heart
want him to live free and long
so i never tell him about the

glances
double takes
stares

gasps
giggles
interrogations

in bathrooms
dressing rooms
hallways

he doesn't know about the

cars screeching
doors exploding
boots chasing

"Damn dyke"
"Fucken dyke!"
"You want to be a man?!
I'll show you who's a man!"

yelled across streets
and in my face

he leaves wife and kids
for the war zone
entrusts me with his prize,
baby blue monte carlo

i cruise mission street
acting as if i bought
the 49ers license plate
pretending my name's
on the title

a lifetime later
a dead man returns
mumbles hello
when he means good-bye

i welcome brother home
feed him cold coronas
and cheap tequila

i drag him to a party
introduce him to a lovely lady
she melts his armor
he asks her to be his wife
he tells me his happy news

i wait for mine

i plan the perfect bachelor party
take him to that jewelry shop on mission
the one with the sign that says:
una mujer sin joyas
es como
una noche sin estrellas

i schedule the fitting for our tuxes
and matching cummerbunds

brother ten-huts me awake.
before his second woman in white,
he turns for the ring

from the last pew,
i reach for my empty pocket
as father hands brother my ring

i charge the couple at the altar
i shove father the imposter
strike brother the wartime zero

i shout
it should've been me!
lord knows it should've been me!

i wasn't the best man
but i was the better man

RICHTER SCALE

Bonnilee Kaufman

The relatives remarked:
"she's too sensitive,
that's why"
I sense
the fissure,
sense
subtle shifts
middle of the night
rickety tectonic plates
rearrange
I hold fast,
onto
edges of my bed, brave knuckled
from
very first tremors
even those minor
less than two point
hardly register on the Richter scale
I sit upright
impeccable
posture on Aladdin's royal blue
gold tasseled magic carpet,
three wishes
ride out the storm

I sense
the fissure
all my gristle
gathers
like a rope of dust

not strong enough to push
plate glass
doors
reflect eruptions
white pustules on lips
line mucus membranes, render
mouth useless
whoever heard of a tongue
uncomfortable
in its den

Lately too thin
skin cracks
I try to bend down
pick up pieces
but my tailbone shifted
duly left
into back pockets
where money used to be
and I worry
literally spend time
contemplating
near-to
homelessness
and what if I
drop
health insurance
since the landlord
raised rent
and even as I
swallow what's prescribed
shove aside

clumps of hair
shedding
wishes gone awry
I still wait for her
to surprise me,
with periwinkle blue hydrangeas.

BLACK VELVET SHAWL

Ronna Magy

I imagine standing in front of her wrapped in a black velvet shawl, trailing silken fringe along my face, under dark eyes, a belly dancer with the glint of gold coins shimmering from waist and hips. From beneath this veiled dance, I look into her eyes, my hips swirling from side to side. In serpentine motion, my hands caress her long hair as though lapping the waves. I bring her in closer, to enchant and beguile, pull her back from the fear of love.

For a while she's lived amidst separation and loss. Away from the feel of velvets and silks, away from a trail of fringe and lace. During this time she's lived in the world of straight men and marriage, children and houses, property and plans. Just as her years in that life grew, that existence was pulled away in divorce, in settlement, in selling the house, in dividing money and goods. Daughters and sons scattered, thrown like dust on the winds. The bang of a judge's gavel and the act, complete. Those years, all those years, she wonders, where did they go?

On a walk near the ocean she hints years ago she was bi. The sexual revolution, the women's movement, and the headiness of those times. After college, she recalls, as we walk on the sand. A girl friend in grad school who became something more. It happened one day while studying, a kiss, and then . . . What was to stop them? The attraction was there.

This, years before her marriage to him. She never told him. He never knew. This man who now no longer understands the woman she is, and only thinks he knows the woman she once was. This older man who now lives with a thirty-year-old, young enough to be his child. This new wife, this woman of younger flesh, filled with desire for him, the "older" man, a man knowing in the ways of the world.

On that warm winter day with waves lapping on shore, water and seashells baubling imprints along edges of sand, amongst washed up trees of sea kelp, she hints she might be interested, and over Chardonnay talks of those days with women, the women's movement, those earlier times. Closes brown eyes and easily smiles. There are her breasts beneath that silken shirt. The way she leans in towards me as she sips on her wine.

I imagine the dance of scarves we will do in bed, the covering and the uncovering of skin. The rub and feel of velvet, of hands on lips on face on cheeks through hair on neck on shoulders on breasts on hips along one leg, and then the other, and in between. I imagine the dance we will do on another wintery day when the motions of our bodies will warm to the notes, attune to the swirling dance of the veils.

WURUNDJERI COUNTRY, MELBOURNE, AUSTRALIA: OUTLAWS UPROOTED

Jean Taylor

L iving in Australia, where the Aboriginal and Torres Strait Islander people have been living for the previous hundred thousand years or more, and knowing that my ancestors on my mother's side had sailed here from Scotland in the nineteenth century and had displaced the people of the Wathaurung, the Woiwurrung and the Gunai/Kurnai language groups, and my father had migrated from Belfast, Ireland in 1927 to live in Latji Latji country, it's no wonder that for most of my life I have felt as if I didn't quite belong.

Add to that the fact that I was brought up and went to school in a small conservative country town and didn't arrive back in Melbourne till the day after I got married at eighteen years of age, two months pregnant, and with a new husband in tow. I was a city person, a Melbournian, and never again would I live in the country, I vowed to myself.

And I didn't, apart from one briefly disastrous time in 1966 which only confirmed my prejudices, till 1979 when I fell in love with a womyn who lived in a small country town in Gippsland. There was nothing for it but to pack up some of my belongings, including my double bed, take my daughter with me and move to live with my lesbian lover in a large house on a hill with her two daughters, leaving my son in my house in Melbourne. Our passionate but ultimately disastrous relationship lasted about eighteen months before I was able to extricate myself, pack up my belongings (my daughter had already moved back to Melbourne to live with her brother and to do her higher school certificate), and move to a friend's house in Melbourne to get my life back together again.

I was divorced and had been a radical feminist in the women's liberation movement for several years before I came out as a lesbian in 1979. I had imagined that by falling in love with a womyn I would automatically become a lesbian and that all would be wonderful. Not so, unfortunately. For starters, at age thirty-five—even though I knew and had worked with many lesbians on collectives over the previous years—I really had no idea how to go about choosing a lover wisely or how to live as a lesbian. It took me several lesbian relationships over a number of years before I was finally able to be more discerning in my choice of lovers, although at no time did I ever stop being attracted to lesbians or doubt that I was a lesbian myself.

Most of the lesbians I knew had known from an early age that they were lesbians, and so had never married or had children. I was therefore unable to identify my own experiences with those lesbians who told stories about coming out in the bars or the young lesbians who had come out in their teens or soon after leaving school. I often had the impression that lesbians like myself who had children and had obviously been in previous partnerships with males were not "real" lesbians and had to somehow prove ourselves. That the lesbian community on the whole didn't particularly like children didn't help matters and the Lesbian Mothers Bridge the Gap Forum was organized in Melbourne in 1984 to address these issues. That my children were teenagers by the time I came out made it easier in a sense, and as the topic never came up, on the rare occasions when it was appropriate to mention them, some lesbians were surprised I had children at all.

Mind you, I am very glad I had my children and I wouldn't have ever given them up for anything, and these days I get enormous satisfaction out of being a grandmother to my four grandchildren, a bonus for all those difficult mothering years if ever there was one.

When I first came out I'd been a radical feminist activist for about seven years which made moving to the country in 1980 where there was no one within cooee distance [calling distance] who was prepared to admit they were dykes very difficult. I'd been working in a women's refuge [shelter for abused women] for the previous two years and had been actively engaged with the Women's Liberation Centre and on a number of other collectives and actions; I missed the lesbian feminist camaraderie and the intense political interactions as well as the sense that I was part of the worldwide women's liberation movement. In the country, where the pub was the focus of social life, I took comfort in the fact that at least my lover and I weren't being physically threatened, although our teenage daughters had to weather some flack at high school, and that by being part of an obvious lesbian couple I was contributing to lesbian visibility.

When we ventured down to Melbourne for some necessary lesbian-feminist input for a week or two, we visited the Kingston Hotel in Richmond which became a lesbian hangout during the 1980s by virtue of the fact that the new licensee was a lesbian. Lesbians sold drinks behind the bar, lesbian-feminists held fundraisers in the downstairs bistro area, and bar dykes held the pool table in the front room. I had naively assumed that with the advent of feminism and the women's liberation movement bar dykes and butch-femme role-playing were passé, and was surprised to discover that wasn't the case at all. The Women's Pub, as it came to be known, gave lesbian-feminists like myself the chance to become friends with some of the bar dykes which went a long way towards giving me an understanding about why bar dykes were hostile towards feminists for criticizing butches and femmes who had no intention of giving up their lifestyles. At the same time, our conversations enabled me to see there were many equally legitimate ways of identifying as a lesbian even though for myself I had long embraced a personal androgynous appearance with my very short hair, no makeup, and overalls.

When sadomasochism became a prominent issue in the early 1990s and I wrote an article explaining my feminist point of view, some sadomasochists stopped speaking to me. As I had come of age as a lesbian, so to speak, and was much more confident in myself as well as my opinions, the fact that they were ignoring me didn't bother me unduly. However, other lesbians who practiced S/M were not so threatened by my views and remained friends of mine. We all seemed to be able to coexist in the same large lesbian community in Melbourne, be present at some of the same lesbian events, and have our articles printed in the same lesbian publication without any overt hostility even if we had diametrically opposing views.

However, over these past ten years or so radical lesbian feminists like myself have not only been effectively silenced by the lesbian and gay media, we've been driven underground for fear of being hauled into the Victorian Civil and Administrative Tribunal (VCAT) for wanting to organize events for lesbians born female. Thanks to the Equal Opportunity Act here in Victoria, it is illegal to discriminate against anyone on the basis of gender or sexual orientation. Transpeople can have their birth certificates altered to reflect their transitioned genital status. This effectively means that if lesbians born female want to get together for our own exclusive wellbeing we do so at our own risk. The organizers of the Lesbian Festival in Victoria in 2004, which was for lesbians born female only, for example, had to cancel the event rather than do battle in court with transpeople who might have won the right to attend. The organizers of Sappho's Party in South Australia in 2006 had to pay $10,000 to defend themselves at the VCAT after a transperson in Sydney complained to the Equal Opportunity Commission that the organizers had advertised the event for lesbians born female only.

This is not to say that radical lesbian-feminists such as myself are unsympathetic to the plight of transpeople. Having lived in this misogynist, racist, and lesbophobic society all my life, I am well aware of the brutality and discrimination that many lesbians, womyn, and girl children live with on a daily basis. I have no doubt at all that transpeople need to be protected by law from the worst excesses of the discriminatory and violent society we live in. I have attended many events, such as Midsumma Carnival and the Word is Out Readings at Melbourne's LGBTIQQ bookstore, Hares and Hyenas, where I am in contact and have spoken with and listened to transpeople, and have read numerous articles in lesbian and gay periodicals where their particular viewpoints are regularly included. I am well aware that transpeople have managed to gain the ear of government and the sympathy of the law to promote their cause in a comparatively short time.

What concerns me as a radical feminist who was born female and raised as a girl is that in order to support the particular rights of transpeople I have been expected to negate my own specific needs. It's as if the rights of transpeople and the rights of lesbians born female are incompatible, which is patently absurd. If it is as impossible for me to deny my own existence as a lesbian born female as it is for a transperson not to transition, then we all need to find a way for every part of the LGBTIQQ community to coexist without negating one section to promote the other. In much the same way that I have no problems with transpeople getting together to discuss their own particular concerns, promoting their views, or being enabled to be heard, I'd like the opportunity to do likewise without fear of someone dobbing me and my friends in to the Equal Opportunity Commission.

After decades of womyn-only consciousness-raising groups where we came up with the theory of feminism and then put these radically new ideas into practice in lesbian and womyn's activist collectives as well as in the way we relaxed, entertained, and sustained ourselves at lesbian dances, concerts, conferences, and festivals, it came as a huge shock to learn that the very core of our cultural and political existence was not only no longer acceptable or valid but was indeed discriminatory and therefore illegal.

Imagine, if you will, what it must be like for a lesbian who has worked long unpaid hours on various collectives as a radical feminist over many decades to make the world a better place to live, and who has been out and proud as a lesbian for over thirty years, to reach her sixties only to discover that she is no longer able to get together with her fellow radical lesbian-feminists because her views about herself and her place in the world are considered unlawful.

I am now in my seventieth year. I am not aligned with those who want marriage rights, as if marriage wasn't one of the more harmful aspects of patriarchy. I think that a womyn's right to control her own body is being insidiously undermined by the push to pay for children to be born through a surrogate mother. Prostitution is seen as an acceptable work choice and the physical and psychological dangers for womyn who are sex workers are ignored. All up, I'm beginning to understand why old people find change difficult when some of the changes we're being asked to embrace are not in our own or anyone's best interests when seen from a radical lesbian-feminist point of view.

One good thing, even though we've been called dinosaurs—some of us prefer Tyrannosaurus Regina (to rhyme with vagina)—for holding on to what many consider outdated views, our radical lesbian-feminist community here in Australia is still sufficiently large enough to be the kind of mutually supportive environment I need to get on with my work and life.

HOMECOMING

Doreen Perrine

S am gazed through the half oval of the plane window. The reflection of her green eyes floated across the surface of the thick glass. The pilot announced a "delay due to foggy conditions." *Am I stuck in a time warp again?*

She nervously raked her fingers through her cropped black hair. Maybe she should have taken Gina's advice and let her lawyer deal with this. After Greg's vicious letter, Sam had immediately phoned Norm Ziegel. He'd warned her to "Strike while the iron's hot" or before Sam's ex-husband could change his mind. "Nicky's father might decide he doesn't want to cut her out of his life, after all," Norm had pointed out. "And you *cannot* relive the nightmare of the custody battle he put you through."

No.

But maybe Gina was right. Norm might have better luck—and much less anxiety—persuading Greg to sign the papers. Still, Sam had scraped together the airfare to settle this once and for all. She had run too far for much too long.

The plane circled, spiralling closer to land. The view split off into a hazy patchwork of the farmlands and woods that clung to the city's border. Sam made out a fragmented outline of her small hometown. It rose into view then, like a backwoods *Brigadoon*, vanished into cloudy mist.

The landscape appeared more urban than Sam recollected. Fresh out of high school and without the vantage point of this bird's-eye view, she'd escaped in Greg's clunky car. She hadn't returned since just after Nicky's birth thirteen years before. She had visited her family with living proof of her motherhood—the chubby-cheeked baby nestled in her arms.

Details, buildings, streets, blinking traffic lights, and the crisscross lines of the ambling highway, materialized like a toy train set. The plane swooped along the stretching runway, rocked, then slowed to a silent halt.

As if she could bolster her jumbled nerves, Sam squeezed the armrest of her window seat.

She clicked off the alarm of the white rental and flung her bag onto the back seat. The moment she merged onto the two-lane highway, she was ambushed by a flood of bitter memories. Her knuckles whitened as she tightly gripped the steering wheel. Her uneasy breath rose and fell in quick, almost spasmodic spurts.

"What the *fuck* am I doing back here?" she muttered, then instantly reminded herself *I can't stop fighting for my daughter!* Even if it meant facing her estranged family.

During the subway ride to LaGuardia Airport, Sam and Gina had lapsed into an absurd debate. Which of their childhoods had been more dysfunctional? Gina had grown up in a Catholic household with a crucifix mounted on the wall of every room. Her Italian American parents had expected her to live at home until she married. A man, of course. She'd equated her eighteenth birthday, the day she had moved out, with resurrection.

For Sam, the crucifix of her Protestant upbringing had been her father's leather strap. For as far back as she could remember, it had draped, a painful icon, above the kitchen table. Hushed whispers, guilty apologies, tiptoeing past the sunken throne of Daddy's armchair had been daily routines. What had Sam's rigid father taught his children other than shameful fear?

Gina had embraced her before the departure gate. "Just don't say *Jesus Christ* like a cuss word down there," she half joked. She'd laughed, kissed Gina, then stepped past the gate. "Tell Nick I'll text her later," Sam called over the shoulder.

What was the point of burdening the kid with more of Greg's twisted rejection? She'd simply told Nicky she was visiting her mother. That much was partly true. She hadn't heard from her mother in over ten years. Like the rest of the family, she'd caved into her husband's demand to cut Sam out of their lives.

Yet, weirdly, she'd once driven the pickup from Kansas to Florida. She'd met Sam on a deserted road outside the trailer park.

"Never tell your father about this." She lowered her voice as if her husband could hear across state lines.

As if to purge her nostrils, Sam exhaled the acrid odor of her father's cigars in the clunky truck. "Don't worry about it, Ma." Sam had exchanged few words with the gruff man over the years.

Her mother's limp cheeks hung like pale washcloths from her drawn face. She handed Sam a white bag imprinted with HAVE A NICE DAY *across it. Through the plastic circle of a yellow smile face, Sam made out a wad of green cash.*

Sam smiled, too. That money would buy her the sweet freedom of a divorce!

"This is what I salvaged of your aunt's life insurance. You were always her favorite," her mother said, grasping Sam's hand with a firm, throbbing grip. A grip that bespoke the earthy farm stock they were descended from. Gritty tooth and nail folk, their people had survived the horror of the Dust Bowl.

"I'm sure Auntie N woulda been happy to see ya outta that loveless marriage."

Was Sam's mother happy?

"I don't need to know 'bout the rest." Her breathy words trailed off into feeble silence.

Nicky, three, trained her big alert eyes on her grandmother, who kissed the girl's forehead. As though she witnessed a memory, Sam's mind flashed to her own toddler years. Her mother had fewer children and had been more attentive then.

Avoiding her mother's woeful face, she stared at the staggered rays of a bowed street lamp. Will you ever accept me as I am? *Sam, who rarely posed questions, longed to ask.*

True to the tacit nature of her closemouthed past, she held her tongue.

She pulled off the highway exit and drove toward the motel on the outskirts of town. The musty dump reminded her of the one in which she and Greg had spent their wedding night.

Another memory, first vague, then painfully vivid, came to mind. She'd been pregnant "out of wedlock," her sister had called it, for four months. After the quickie church service, Greg had clapped his rough hands.

"Fifty bucks and it's all said and done." He thumped her back as they drove to the motel with a buzzing VACANCY sign. "We'll do it up proper one day," he said.

His brusque thump felt like that of a buddy teammate for a sports game as if to urge Sam, Go Team! Go Marriage!

"It's not a 'proper' wedding I want, Greg," Sam mumbled in quiet protest.

She stared at the cheap ring that encircled her finger. Wasn't it one more link in the chain she had forged over the past eighteen years of her stifled life?

What had she wanted? Not until Gina's decisive question three years later, "What *do* you want, baby?" had Sam begun to claim her squelched desires. Desires she'd resuscitated like a drowning child who could barely breathe—let alone speak.

She tapped the bell that dipped with the warped wood of the reception desk. She checked into a dingy single room, then shuffled, her feet dragging, toward Main Street. Greg's lawyer had refused to divulge his phone number and address. While her hometown had grown, Sam needed to find her eldest sister.

And there was only one place for that.

As though they would topple one another, row houses tilted in a lean-to, domino effect. Even trees and flowers that lined the crackled sidewalk looked withered. Had the shabby town ever recovered from the Great Depression?

Sam patted the bulge of papers in the pocket of her corduroy jacket. Then she lifted her chin and marched forward. With her lengthy stride, she felt like a giant, not only in her tall stature, but internally. She no longer felt the eerie, alien sense the prying stares of townspeople had once evoked. *Ghosts*, she shrugged at a passing couple, *I'm strolling down a street of ghosts.* Did she even know anyone anymore—classmates who'd snubbed her? A teacher who had belittled her quiet misfit nature? She simply wouldn't, couldn't have joined in cheerleading their one-size-fits-all world.

If someone rambling along that sidewalk had recognized her, Sam didn't care. She had returned with the sole driving purpose to win full custody of her daughter. Nothing more.

She stopped before a small brown church and stared at its roughly hewn stone façade. In contrast to the flimsy wooden buildings, the church stood out like the white letters on its black message board. *GOD DWELLS HERE!*

Sam rolled her eyes at the sign. Then she sidestepped a straggle of church ladies descending the steps. She cut across the trimmed lawn and clapped the brass knocker of a dull gray rectory. A scrawny boy, about Nicky's age, opened the door and gaped up. Could this be her nephew? Sam hadn't set eyes on her sister's kids in so long, she didn't know.

"Is Ellie Wilson home?" Sam asked plainly.

After shaking his head with a gloomy look, the boy slipped out of sight. Sam crossed her arms and braced herself for the moment of reckoning. Her sister was sure to light into her with some hellfire sermon.

A short thin man with a pinched nose and rolled-up white sleeves appeared on the threshold. "Mrs. Parker isn't home. Can I help you?"

Sam recognized the older version of her brother-in-law but said nothing. Then she realized she'd asked for her sister by her maiden name. "I'm her sister, Samantha."

"I thought so." He scrunched his angular face and studied her with a tight frown. "You've changed . . . so much since we last saw you."

He seemed reluctant to invite her inside. Well, she hadn't expected a hearty welcome.

"Yes, Reverend, it was some time . . . and another lifetime ago," Sam said, instinctively glancing at her watch. She had no time for chit chat with long lost relatives who preached against her *sinful lifestyle*.

"I just need to ask Ellie to help me find my ex-husband. We have some . . . loose ends to tie up." She hesitated to reveal too much. This was between her and Greg, after all.

"She's visiting a sick parishioner down the block. I'll phone her." As if he expected Ellie to materialize out of air, he shot a furtive look around the doorframe. "In the meantime, you might want to visit the graveyard."

Sam turned toward the tree-hedged graveyard behind the church. "That's okay. I'll wait here." She could hardly "visit" the cold ground where they had buried her kindest relative. Auntie N.

"If you like." The reverend shrugged. "But there's somebody you may want to say 'goodbye' to." He disappeared behind the threshold, then shut the door.

"What the hell?" Sam spun on her boot heels.

Someone had died, that was clear. Could her brother-in-law have meant Sam's aunt, buried fifteen years before? As if in a hypnotic trance, Sam stepped slowly. A gnawing panic seized her and she picked up her pace. She meandered along the jagged rows of worn dirt paths. Pink-white petals from a flowering lilac littered the ground. Its wings spread, an angel with a chipped, half-head knelt above an eroded limestone slab.

Sam scanned the gravestone names with terse glances. Then she stopped before a patch of weeds that veiled a scant white grave. She took a deep breath, then stepped up. *Nicole Beardan*, Sam's daughter's namesake, was incised into the arc of the unadorned headstone.

The tickling breeze that whisked Sam's bangs stirred a vague recollection. Hadn't her spinster aunt often tousled her stringy, unkempt hair when Sam was a kid? She smiled. Fond, the best really, girlhood memories of her loving aunt played freely in her mind. No coffin could seal them up.

She faced the stone a moment longer, then turned her head. Her eyes widened at a polished stone with a wreath of plastic daisies clinging to its base. A shiver of shock pulsed through Sam and she stumbled, clutching the headstone to steady herself.

"Christ!" She gripped her forehead as she crumpled to her knees. Below the name *Grace Wilson*, Sam scrutinized the dates and gasped. Her mother had died a year before at the age of fifty-two.

"Why, Ma?" The moment she'd posed it, Sam knew the answer to her sobbing question. Her mother had borne seven children and raised five. Motherhood had whittled away, first, her youth, then her increasingly frail health. Had she given birth so often to placate Sam's overbearing father? Or had unchecked childbirth filled some gaping inner void?

Sam would never know—or understand.

She remembered her sister's words during Nicky's birth.

"God is the light in each new baby's eyes."

Ellie's grating voice grew almost as torturous as Sam's contractions. Had she sat through too many of her preacher husband's prayer meetings?

"And to think, some women condemn themselves to a motherless world." Ellie sharply arched her dark brow at Sam.

Sam gripped the bar of the hospital bed and heaved herself into an upright position. "In case you haven't noticed, Ellie, I'm having this baby!" she cried. "What's the damn problem?" "There was a time when you were struggling with other options," Ellie replied in a low but unmistakably haughty voice.

Ever since she'd married the Reverend Dwight Parker Ellie's religious fervor had wearied even their churchgoing parents. After four years of marriage, she had borne two children and was pregnant again. Where she toted her kids like a brood of saintly clones, her godly motherhood was unnerving.

Ellie whipped out a black leather pocket Bible from her purse like a book of magic spells. Sam groaned as her sister clutched the book to her bosom. Here comes the soapbox sermon, *Sam thought drearily.*

"Each child is just so special to Jesus, Samantha." As if she unearthed some profound cryptic meaning, Ellie carefully enunciated every word.

"Just being born doesn't make you special," Sam answered dryly. With the turmoil raging inside her womb, she hardly cared what her sanctimonious sister thought. "If this child is special," she rubbed her bulging belly, "it'll be because of who *this child becomes."*

A sudden shadow loomed across the granite headstone. As if the memory had summoned her presence, Ellie stood over Sam.

"So here you are."

Sam got to her feet.

Ellie was dressed simply in a girlish pink jumper and a paisley blouse. Her jet black hair was pinned back in a taut, fistlike bun. Though she had changed little, her frown appeared stiffer, as it if had been glued onto her face.

Ellie hugged her sister briskly, then stepped, just as briskly, back. "I see you found Ma," she said through pursed lips.

"Why didn't you tell me she died?" Sam struggled to keep her churning temper in check. "I needed to mourn her, too." *Mourn,* she thought with an aching throb, *what I lost and what I never had.*

Ellie hung her head. "It was a family decision."

Sam spied the pronounced look of guilt that crossed her sister's face.

"We felt it was best to leave you out of it."

Her words seemed to morph the soft April breeze into an icy wind.

"She was my mother, too!" Sam cried into her palms. "How could you just decide to leave me 'out of it'?" Tears stung her eyes. She wiped them on the cuff of her denim shirt, then threw back her head. The cloudy sky—anything—was better than meeting her sister's stony gaze.

"She was very sick, Samantha, and knowing you had taken up with that . . . *woman.*" Ellie shuddered dramatically. "It was like you already died to her . . . to all of us."

"Please!" Sam fluttered her hands. "*Must* you use our dead mother to prop up your religion? Is your God so merciless . . . and that much of a crutch?" she snapped.

In the tense silence that followed, Sam recalled something. Although she'd promised their mother to never tell their father, it was high time her sister knew. "Ellie," she softened her tone, "Ma helped me . . . gave me Auntie N's money to divorce Greg."

"Impossible!" As if their mother had spoken from underground, Ellie cast her eyes toward the grave.

Sam shrugged sadly. "Maybe you didn't know Ma as well as you imagine. She loved me enough to help me make a better life for myself."

Just then, Sam felt a sure, if unspoken, connection to the woman buried at her feet. She squeezed her sister's shoulder. "Ma wanted me to buy my freedom from what she called a loveless marriage." Sam reflected on her relationship with her own child. "The best I can give *my* Nicky," she said, "is to help her find . . . and honor herself in this mixed-up world." She paused, then met her sister's gaping expression. "Just like *our* mother did for me," she added.

Sam thought back to the joyful first days of motherhood. She'd delighted in Nicky's gurgling smile and in how she squeezed a fist of small curling fingers in her mouth. Those intimate moments—cradling and breastfeeding, or simply humming her baby to sleep—had moved Sam deeply. She forced a crooked smile. "Mother love can be an exceptional thing," she murmured. That much understanding, if nothing else, she and her sister shared.

Mutely, Ellie blinked at Sam. Then, like a stirring pool of stagnant water, her deep green eyes appeared troubled.

"You've disgraced your family."

The bland judgment seemed to drop from Ellie's lips with a flat thud. Had the youthful vigor of diehard convictions faded from her voice? Maybe she had finally tired of mouthing holier-than-thou platitudes.

Though Ellie's harsh statement might have riled Sam, thoughts of her aunt, her child, *her* Gina, and even her estranged mother calmed her. *Spirit Women,* she thought of the feminine forces that had guided her path to a more promising life.

"Listen," Sam thrust up her right hand like a stop sign, "I didn't come all this way to hear a fire and brimstone speech."

"Why did you come?" Ellie asked with a half-hearted shrug.

"I only want to keep my daughter in my life." Sam's pitch rose to a feverish plea, "*Ellie*, you're my sister and a mother yourself." If she had to stoop to begging, she would. "I can't—" She stopped short of delving into the agonizing custody battle she'd endured. "Greg needs to quit acting like the father he has never been to our child. Puberty's tough enough. He can't keep toying with that kid's emotions!"

Ellie's gaze shifted from the gravestone to Sam. Like a puppet whose strings had been abruptly cut, she flopped her head. Her arms hung limply at her sides. "What can I do about that?"

"I want . . . *need* Greg to sign over his custodial rights," Sam said, stepping toward her sister. "He wrote that because of Nicky's choice to live with me and Gina, he wants nothing more to do with her. I need to make that stick." She gripped her sister's slumped shoulder. "He's a member of your husband's congregation now. You must know about that nasty letter he sent Nick." Sam paused, then whispered the dreaded question, "Did *you* help him write it?"

"The man isn't illiterate." Ellie bit her lower lip and averted her eyes with a sheepish sideways look.

It was a hangdog gesture they, Sam and all of her siblings, had enacted before their stern father. But they had been children then.

"Greg doesn't want to see you," Ellie said in a trailing whisper. "I need to honor his wishes."

"Umm, I think I can live with never seeing him again." Sam smirked. "But I'd like you to honor a wish of mine." She drew the folded papers out of her pocket. "Get that *literate* man to sign these, will you?" Sam handed her sister the papers. "My daughter has made her parent of choice clear. And it's not him."

She squatted, kissed her fingers, and pressed them to the inscriptions of their mother's and aunt's names. Without another word, she marched back to the motel and packed her bag.

Then she checked out and headed for the airport.

She nibbled what Nicky would have called despicable airplane food. Since her thirteenth birthday a month before, despicable, like atrocious and mindboggling, had become a pet word. As Gina had observed, "Pubescent girls have a knack for hyperbole."

Sam handed the tray back to the stewardess. "Thanks anyway," she mumbled with a polite smile. Despite her gnawing hunger, she'd wait until she got home.

Sam glanced at her watch. Happily, time seemed to speed up in a kind of fast forward mode. She'd hopped on a direct flight to New York and would arrive a day early. Just in time for Gina's Sunday night pasta.

The back and forth motion of the rocking plane lulled Sam into a heavy slumber. Images, a lake, a child, a long link of heavy chains, jostled like shifting puzzle pieces in her dream.

Golden pebbles lined the opposite bank of a stretching lake. She stood naked with her hands covering her pubes. Dragging rusty chains were shackled to her hands and feet. A clamoring anonymous crowd with upheld fists encircled her. What crime, Sam's mind spun with frazzled wonder, did I commit to spark this hateful judgment? She couldn't distinguish their angry babble from waves splashing against the shoreline. But she made out their reference to the water body as a "lake of fire."

"Of eternal damnation?" Sam asked, thinking back to her childhood Sunday School lessons. She squinted at the lake her judges

backs were turned against. The one she faced. There were no flames. Only a clear, serene blue.

Sam made out a small smiling figure on the other shore. The figure, a little girl in a beelike yellow and black striped bathing suit waved. Sam started to wave, but was bound by the clasping chains that gripped her wrists and ankles.

Suddenly, the chains vanished as Sam felt, more than heard, the girl shout, "There is no judgment here!"

As the lapping waves called to Sam, the crowd disappeared. She walked to the bank where gentle ripples licked her bare toes. At the muddy shore she stepped down until, shoulder high in water, she swam. Folding her arms over into each stroke, she saw that the child she moved toward was her daughter.

Like a prehistoric life form emerging onto land, Sam crawled out on all fours. On shore, she gazed into the child's big green eyes and was taken aback.

Instead of her daughter, Sam faced her own mother as a girl.

She flung her arms around her child-mother who repeated in a tender murmur, "There is no judgment here."

A restless week followed Sam's return. She barely slept, and despite Nicky's urging her to "chill out already," Sam repeatedly checked the mailbox. She stared bleary-eyed at the answering machine, longing for a message—from her sister or her lawyer. It didn't matter which.

Finally, a white cardboard envelope arrived by courier. Sam quickly tore off the stringy seal of its red strip. Ellie's tight cursive looped across the pink Post-it note stuck to the papers. On it, she had written simply, *For Ma's sake, I honored your wish.*

She flipped wildly through the pages for a single scratchy signature. Sure enough, Greg had signed over full custody of their daughter to Sam!

She whooped for joy and kissed Gina's smiling mouth. They giggled in a girlish chorus as Sam spun Nicky around in her arms.

QUEER ASIAN AUSTRALIAN MIGRATION STORIES: INTIMATE ARCHIVES BIG AND SMALL

Audrey Yue

In 1991 I was the first Asian lesbian in Australia to lodge a same-sex migration permanent residency application with my then partner under the new interdependency visa category.[1] Interdependency visas are for people who have an interdependent—usually samesex—relationship with an Australian citizen or permanent resident, and the relationship must be genuine and continuing, and involve a mutual commitment to a shared life together. At that time we had been lovers for three years. We first met as undergraduate students in Perth, and she moved to Melbourne with me when I was offered a postgraduate scholarship to begin my doctoral study. We wanted to be together, and were overjoyed when the new visa class was introduced. It was as if our relationship had finally secured a legitimacy that was no longer at the whim of ministerial discretion or needing the extremity of humanitarian justification. As the first country to introduce such a visa category, Australia was quickly recognized worldwide for its progressive sexual law reform.

It took more than six months for us to prepare our application. To create the narrative of our relationship, to document the archive of our intimacy, we had to look back to the three years in Perth. Did we have any Christmas cards or utility bills addressed to the both of us at the same addresses? Like many students living in shared houses, we were transient tenants. Were there

---

1   Asia is a vast geographical region with disparate histories and differential modernities. I use the term "Asian" as it is usually mobilized in Australia: as a convenient umbrella category, a collective noun to refer to people from southeast Asia. It is important to note that in public discourse, Asian often connotes a racial stereotype constructed through the presumed inferiority of skin color and facial features.

photos taken of us together as a couple, with friends and family, in particular, with my partner's family in the southwestern Australian town of Albany where we visited a few times a year, during almost every term break? What about all the letters we wrote each other when I returned to Singapore every summer?

I began to obsessively compile the chronology of our lives together, through greeting cards, love letters, house bills, family photos. I hoarded all types of used and stamped envelopes—it didn't matter where they were from, as long as both our names were on the front—and meticulously organized them according to postal dates in order to show the duration of our connection. This was one part of the archive enterprise—only couples that have been together more than two years are eligible to apply. The other part of the archive enterprise was getting it right. We needed external corroboration, better yet if from a diversity of social networks, to show we were an out, proud, and well-adjusted couple. From friends, community groups, colleagues and employers, we shamelessly requested statutory declarations that verified the normality of our love and the authenticity of our commitment. We needed to demonstrate a narrative of public intimacy: a kind of public intimacy valued – as heterosexual love is – for monogamy and longevity.

Two years after the application was lodged, the same process of documentation was again required. Provide an update of your relationship, we were told. By this time, I had begun to internalize the fetish of this archive, never throwing away any envelopes, keeping all receipts and, most of all, always insisting, from any authorities big and small, on the proper "address" of our coupledom. The migration bureaucracy had come to institutionalize my life and shape my sexual conduct into a form they recognized. In the 1990s, before post-AIDS and postgay, before the ubiquity of the Internet and social media, and before marriage equality, these straightening and universalizing practices, through the intimate enterprise of our archive, became the new public technologies that fixed the portrait of our affection.

I was considered a "test case" by the Immigration Department, which had yet to draft clear guidelines to assess same-sex applications. During the five years that I waited to successfully attain permanent residency, my passport was assigned numerous border passes. When my international student visa expired, I was repeatedly granted many variations of temporary visas. They ranged from three days, to four weeks, to six months. On my final visit to the immigration processing office, the officer who examined my two sealed passports was quite shocked to see the full range of stamps and stickers haphazardly strewn between the pages, where the expired passport was glued to the current passport to maintain proof of my extended temporary residency. After attaching the subclass "155" permanent residency label on the page, he looked up, and, with a tinge of nonchalant sadness, told me he had never seen so many visa categories given to any one person before. At that moment, my anxiety-laden relief was immediately overtaken and dulled by pain.

Thinking back, I did not know offshore applications from Asia, and onshore applications from Asians, took longer than those from ETA-approved countries, especially if from the European or North American continents. I have to admit it crossed my mind when I heard that an acquaintance, a white Canadian national, was successfully granted the same visa in less than two years, although I could not say for sure. Many years later while sharing my migration story with my friend R, a Malaysian Chinese Muslim butch who also arrived and resettled through the same means, I realized s/he also waited more than seven years to be granted permanent residency, and the pain I had felt gradually turned my archive into a dossier of trauma, not caused by displacement but fractured by the institutionalization of migration.

As a temporary resident with no welfare and health rights and a partner who was an international graduate film student on a scholarship with no welfare and health rights either, I turned to local gay and lesbian activism hoping I could do something to speed up the visa waiting time. In Melbourne, I became involved with the Gay and Lesbian Immigration Task Force and the multicultural gay and lesbian community group. I worked with seasoned gay bureaucrats, lobbied alongside lipstick lesbians, marched with Chinky pride, and participated in multiple suburban kiss-ins. This was the Zeitgeist of queer coalitional politics in Australia, inspired and influenced by similar mandates in Europe and the U.S. During this period, and especially in the post-9/11 decades to follow, Australia was in the throes of a conservative government characterized by a backlash towards Asians. Asian migration was cut back with the introduction of new border "protection" policies. Samesex migration, however, flourished with gay and lesbian Asian migrants making up the largest successful group in this visa class. Between 1994 and 2007 for example, there were seven thousand five hundred visas issued, and more than half of these issued to Asians.[2]

Key to these flows of sex and people is the institutionalization of an intimate archive—big or small, mainstream or subcultural—of queer Asian migration to Australia. Through migration policies, sexual law reforms and public health programs, from within the official genre formats of relationship dossiers and behavioral surveillance statistics, as well as across the narratives that exceed the vernacular aesthetics of media and epistolary cultures, this archive tells the stories of queer Asian mobility, as well as the governance of Asian migration in national symbolic economies. Like my own story, and the many stories traversed by the intersections of my journey, this period has been both liberating and regulating. Even now after two decades, I still carry my archive box from house to house, lover to lover, as a material remnant of its intimate mobility.

---

2   See Audrey Yue, "Same-Sex Migration in Australia: From Interdependency to Intimacy," *GLQ* 14: 2–3 (2008), 239–262.

FAIRY GODMOTHER

SMoore

Who knows
What happens to old dykes?
(Who knows, who cares?)
They turn into furniture
Occasionally chairs
(the chair you are sitting on
may be your old maid aunt.)
They hang themselves
In closets
Singly, or in pairs
Like out-of-style
Tweed suits.

When I grow old
I'll be skinny mean and bold
They'll be no more juice
To squeeze from yellow bones
My lips will be thin
As onion skin
I'll be too stiff
To twist and turn inside out
Like a casual glove
(no more of that weird inversion, Love.)

When I grow old
I'm going home (never more to roam)
I'll rattle around in my house
Like a bristly broom
I'll stop plucking my whiskers

And grow a beard.
I'll cackle like a cartoon,
Stuff a black dildo in my pants
Maybe learn how to fly
Water my geraniums at midnight
And kiss my mirror
Goodbye.

ENCOUNTERS ON THE BORDER

Joan Nestle

I *know to most readers these West Brunswick street names will have no meaning, but they are the daily boundaries of my life now, having resettled in Melbourne, Australia in 2002 at age 62 to be with my Australian partner, Dianne Otto. These are small streets, short avenues.*

The 19th Century Bluestone Laneway behind Our Home, Originally Used by Horse-Drawn Wagons to Pick up the Night Soil.

"Lady," she said, her face old and worried, one hand leaning on the wooden gate, "Will you help me? You speak Greek?"

No. I'm sorry. What is it? I said.

"Come in," she motioned to the path leading to her wood-framed worn house.

I can't, pointing to my bags filled with things that needed to go into the refrigerator. I saw she had a pen in her hand.

"Can you write English," she asked.

Yes.

"Please. Write this for me." I took the pen and leaned on the top of the low brick wall that fronted her house.

Yes.

"Write, please. Letitia, do not go away. I have to go to the chemist. I will not be long. Do not go away, please!"

As she haltingly said her words, her worry at losing her moment with a friend became more and more evident. Do not worry, I said. See, I am going to use an exclamation point to make sure she does not go away. I showed her every word I had written, pointing to each word. She looked and listened as if a life line was being drawn for her. "God bless you," she said. Thank you. Thank you.

Fitzgibbon Avenue

"Giovana, come in, come in." Anna opens the screen door and leads me down the corridor that runs from the front to the back of her house.

"Where's Dianna, at work, good, good. I just want everything to be alright."

Before we reach the kitchen, she turns off into one of the immaculate bedrooms, "Here, I want to show you my mother." On the tall chest of drawers stands a group of fading sepia-toned photographs. A woman from another time locks eyes with me, hair severely drawn back, hands folded over her apron, arms bare. "Mia madre, strong woman, hard working woman." Anna holds the aging image in her own seventy-four year old, work-hardened hands . "I miss her so, Giovana, so many years, and I miss her. She died over there and I could not get to see her. So sad, so sad." Anna stands with her hand over her heart. I know over there is a small town in Calabria. Over forty five years ago, Anna came to Australia to work in the textile factories, raised her children here. I say words about how hard it is to leave one's family, thinking of how Anna always asks me who did I leave behind. We stand in silence looking at the faces of her history, encased in silver frames. Once I walked down steep streets that led to the sea, once I sang my language, once I felt those hands brush tears off my face. Now what can I do?

The Australian Anna returns, rubs her eyes, come now and have some coffee. Anna is clear, life was too hard in Italy. Her sorrow is stern but everlasting.

Dawson Street

What does change of worlds bring us? "No matter how long I am here," says Mr. Phrom, "I will still long for Saigon...like you for New York." The night is dark and Mr. P has to get up at dawn to chop and simmer in the kitchen of the Vietnamese restaurant on the High Street . We laugh, an odd couple, this small wiry man, always a lit cigarette in his hand, who so loves his family and his god that he barely has time for his other passion, music—and me, stumbling my way through this new world I found myself in when I turned sixty two. The late night tram clatters alongside us, on its way down Dawson to Westgarth Street. I had been visiting with the Phroms in their Sunshine home, a growing Vietnamese residential neighborhood. We speak of our longing for bustling cities as we drive through empty streets. And when he says again, Saigon, with a puff of smoke, I am flooded with memories I have no right to have—the intrigues of a war-torn city, the sounds of a cosmopolitan humid city fighting for its life, thin work-worn farmers and laughing frightened soldiers. The longing for urbanities—the thick flow of life through rivers of streets that speak of known histories. Tumults of lost sounds, different but vibrant, become stars in our night sky.

Grantham Street

I walk to the shops to buy bird seed for our visiting wild parrots and a chicken for our soup. On the way home, I pause to cross the street and a tall old woman in a blue jumper and white skirt, a graying little shepherd-mix by her side, starts to talk to me. The streets are empty now, as they often are, and the morning air is fresh.

"I am ninety-two you know and I was born right here on Grantham street all those years ago. I don't believe in multiculturalism," she looks down at me and says, her tongue moving between her two front teeth. "In my day the Scandinavians lived over there", and she points up the street, and "the Germans lived over there, that's my family, high German," she points down the street—"but we were Australians, this new lot, they never want to fit in but they sure do want everything else." I know from my own limited knowledge of West Brunswick's history that "this new lot", the Lebanese, the Italians, the Vietnamese have been living here for over fifty years.

"What's your name," she asks suddenly.

Joan. And yours?

"Wyn."

I wonder how after commenting on the bird seed overflowing my green bag the very next thing she needed to say to someone on this morning was her dislike of the old change in her neighborhood. She went on speaking to me for a half hour, telling me of her life as a public servant, about her mother's friendship with Emily Pankhurst back in Manchester. The years stretch out around us, almost a century. Then she introduces me to her dog who is growing impatient, "This is Gemina, saved her, no one else wanted her, she is the nervous type."

I have never seen Wyn and Gemina on the street again.

Fitzgibbon Avenue

Last night at one o'clock in the morning, La Professoressa, la mia Dianna, left for Goa, India, to give a paper at a conference. So often our relationship has been this way: I catch her between nations, her joy. Oh darling, we spoke last night on Singapore lines, as we have spoken through oceans so many times before, from Cuba, your voice came to me, from Cambodia and The Basque Country, from Beijing and Kiev, from Belgrade and Fiji, from

Cape Town and New York. I now the permanent emigree. My day starts early, Cello missing you already and wanting his breakfast. Because of drought conditions, we can only water gardens twice a week in the early morning so I begin the rounds, a short woman in her nightgown in the dawn of an early summer day. As I walk down the side of the house to water the tree fern, Anna calls out to me, thinking I am you, "Buongiorna, Dianna, come stai?" [how are you?]

"Buongiorno, Anna. It is me, Giovana, Joan, Di is away, in India. The unspoken words, I am alone.

A pause and over the old wood fence, I see the top of her broom knocking down spider webs.

"Good morning, Joan—I am here, if you need anything, I am here. I am here.

Grazie, Anna.

Encounters at the borders are often an exchange of maps, of requests and disappointments, of crucial translations, of tired hands holding up papers, photographs, hopes. Listen carefully and you will hear histories singing or lamenting, you will hear myriad lonelinesses knowing they are forever and yet one more step, one more step into a new history. On my new old streets, I walk as an aging lesbian, a woman with that American accent, with that Jewish hair, my own left behinds—a black and white picture of the archives filling my New York apartment, a snapshot of Georgia Brooks, Arisa Reed and Mabel Hampton clustered together in conversation during an At Home night, my family, all gone now, in their own frames. I hold on to Anna's words, "Giovana, I am here, I am here" and know that the borders demand such kindness, such dedication to those almost unknown. Thank you, thank you...

CONSTELLATIONS

Yasmin Tambiah

I.

In the hours between midnight and the dawn, the sea draws down the stars. Not all, but enough to drape the waves with luminescence. The Captain knows this. On nights without sleep, when the wind drops, and rivulets of salt leak through skin to join the ocean's spray, the Captain has marvelled. This is not a phenomenon in the seas off the Captain's home, an island far away to the east, beyond the Cape of Good Hope and lost dreams, in the real Indies —the ones that white men thought they'd reach by going west. It is, instead, a feature of the waters between the great continent of Africa and the other land mass in the direction of the sun's setting, particular to the currents that wash the islands whose old names disappeared with their slaughtered peoples.

The Captain runs guns, trading for them with whites who slit each other once they've ripped the skin off black backs for sugar. The Captain, versatile in many tongues, and charming, never explains where the guns go. For a few days each month, near the full moon, the Captain goes ashore on a windward isle to a small house on a cliff. It is looked after by an old woman, skilled in the healing arts of her Kalinago and Yoruba blood lines. The people are afraid of her. Their distance suits both magician and mapper of the sea.

One night, when the wind is high and clouds mob the moon, there's knocking on the door. The tall figure outside limps in, soles split on serrated rock. While the Old Woman prepares a balm, the Captain cleans the blood with tepid water soft with herbs. The Captain recognizes the other's name. This gunrunner's clients are few—all braiding dreams of freedom, an end to manacles and laboring for others. The guns are gifts towards that vision.

The visitor watches the Captain, the assured yet gentle tending of the wounds, and suddenly awakens: this one's like me.

Under care of the Old Woman the visitor stays until the healing is complete. The Captain and the visitor talk freely, admitting to the guises they both take to do their work in a time when heroes are not women, women are not free, and freedom and dark skin are incompatible.

The visitor leaves with the Captain's promise to deliver cargo to her island, the one the hurricanes shun.

For the first time in this business the Captain is afraid.

For the first time she is afraid of loss.

Because, for the first time, there is another who should watch with her the sea draw down the stars, in the hours between midnight and the dawn.

II.

People are the stories they leave behind. There are stories that own the Captain and the Captain's own stories about origins. It is said one night a great gale blew an unmarked ship off course and the tired waves spat out the Captain. In island lore, filled with vain sea monsters and ravenous spirits of the deep, *that* was too tame a telling. So the Old Woman cast one about that a beautiful sprite caressing the waves rescued the Captain going down for the third time and would have scored a fine dinner had not the Old Woman been out throwing nets for her supper and snared both sprite and human and the sprite merged with the human to escape, which is why the Captain is a little strange at full moon and needs to drift back to the windward isle.

The Captain's own telling is as bare as fish bones stripped clean by an eagle of the seas. Traveling trade currents along the Indian Ocean and Arabian Sea, an uneventful trip overland after passing up the Gulf of Aden and the Red Sea and then a quiet float across the Mediterranean and a bit of a mishap with weather in the Atlantic and then, yes, there was a rescue.

But the sea eagle, full of fish, knows otherwise.

In the waters of the real Indies, on an island shaped like a tear drop, lived a king. He was not of that land but acquired it through dynastic accident. When he ascended to the throne the land was his and not his. Two waves of marauding white regiments had already stripped the isle of cinnamon, and anchored in its harbors to command the world. The third spread its red plague completely, shipping the wretched king to the diamond in its imperium, sending him home and not home. With the royal entourage went an advisor, his wife, and two children. The advisor drew his genealogies from the People of the Lion, devourers of the island's indigenes, and the clan of the Cholas whose seafaring kings plundered the Garuda archipelagos far to the east.

Of the children it was said that both were sons. On nearing adulthood, with offers of marriage flowing from noble hopefuls, the younger disappeared. A greying ship's captain in Madras, bound for the trading ports of the Arabian peninsula, acquired a brooding youth tongue-loose in five languages and learned in the atlas of the stars. Startled by the youth's ferocious knife-play the old man, used to pliant male flesh, kept his distance, making the youth his protégé instead. The sailor absorbed quickly the tricks of the sea, the turns of the tide, the moods of men, and in each place of stopping, the stories. The sailor found berth on other ships, impressing captains with interpretations, negotiations, and weapons skill, and soon was one of them.

In time, the new captain is in the Atlantic. It is the season of hurricanes, the first days of calm belying the furies to be. A mile out of the windward isles the spectacular blowing and roiling hook the Captain's ship, drag it down, the waves like fearful arms of fabled creatures. The Captain drinks the sea, swinging between known world and the world to be, and awakens bloodied on rocks with the ship's pieces.

An old woman, skilled in the healing arts of her peoples, walks the rocks as she does after every storm—and finds the Captain.

Undressing the Captain to dress the wounds is an undressing.
The Old Woman smiles, knowing this is a story she will keep.

III.

People are the stories they make anew. The Captain's visitor
releases them a little at a time like a ball of twine knotted at one
end to a raft bearing the will to freedom. The Rebel's tales are not
borne on neat history bifurcated into white masters and black
slaves, sutured with coloured in-betweens. The people on the island
that hurricanes shun arrived on waves rolling in the compromises
of imperial games played far away—one colonizer drawing from
another to counter a third, island hopping island crossing island
drowning—white masters, black slaves, free blacks, free coloreds,
black slaves of free coloreds, black slaves of free blacks. Owning
slaves owning land; a class act even when déclassé from whites. A
family story, a familiar burden. And the boundaries of class, as of
nations, being drawn on the bodies of women.

Against this inheritance the Rebel turns. And falls into favor
with the island's new misfortune where any shade of color is
reviled.

Slave revolts crisscross these waters. A matter of guns, ordering
rage, and carrying secrets. Maroon Wars. Fédon's rebellion. Bussa's
revolt. Even on this staid island the plottings. An old man hobbling.
A crazy-talking simpleton. Tailor, tinker, sailor, spy; who's that
passing the soldiers by?

In the Naparimas one afternoon a peddler dealing gloriously
colored cloth visits a plantation one hundred slaves strong and is
fed in the main kitchen. In this mess of disdain the exact hue of
the peddler's skin is irrelevant—but it is not white. The household's
women are smitten with the wares and gracious conversation. No
one suspects otherwise. The peddler winks at the houseboy who
gestures to the parlor maid who runs to the cook who instructs the
kitchen hand. The overseer and guards sleep heavily that night.
By dawn there are twenty slaves fewer and a cold hearth in the

great house. Someone talks of seeing a strange ship in a cove past midnight. The soldiers search for a peddler of fine fabric. And find nothing.

In Port of Spain there's a tavern brawl. The Governor's paymaster is found dead. Nobody knows if the man was a regular, or if it was a single night's misfortune. His keys are missing. The troops' payroll is lost. The port's black prostitutes and colored rag pickers dine well for a week. Tailor, tinker, sailor, thief; who's that snatching the soldiers' beef?

The legends grow as long as a ball of twine.

In time the Rebel hears of a sea captain who runs guns at no charge for rebellion, and looks for passage to the next island. The Atlantic surges between. A smooth ride for a sea turtle, for others a question of helmsman's skill and reading the clouds. In the history of navigation the Rebel's crossing scores no mention. But the rocks are unkind on the upward climb.

The Rebel is luck's beloved. The Old Woman binds her feet. There is the promise of guns. And an unintended discovery about the Captain.

The Rebel is luck's beloved. The Captain braids her heart. But this is, as yet, a peripheral knowing.

The Rebel is luck's beloved. The return is uneventful. The ball of twine grows.

IV.

People are the stories in their telling. In the caverns of the sea, curl the keepers of memory and guardians of the deep, releasing their tales for offerings: galleys that floundered, caches of gold, bones of explorers, and souls lost in slave ships; long canoes that longing could not draw down playing tag with dragon's mouth and serpent's jaw to row their distances, trading, raiding, settling across the Antilles; Kalinago fury at ravaging white men stewed with Maroon rage and gunpowder familiar as cassava bread in the blood in dawns always fetid with sweat and despair on an island named for a last Moorish kingdom defying a young empire grasping at its intrepid new world.

Young girl's hopes netted Fédon's dreaming—white running so black and colored could own their own stories. Papa stepping with rebels, burning great houses and sugar mills, tripping troops; Papa hanged in the market square, free black and slave and colored together. And the young girl seeing.

The Old Woman remembers.

Mama working her hands raw in the day, eyes blinding slowly at night to a needle and shadows and solitary candle. The girl sorting cloth scraps for stories, braiding daughter with mother and women before them. And wisdoms of plants and healing following, Yoruba tricks, Kalinago cunning, knowledge of lunar and human faces, love and yearning and the fiction of races.

In time the young woman turns heads in the market square—and not just for her beauty. By day her potions and pouches are prized for women's business and fretting babes, stomach aches and phlegmy chests, and shy boys wanting to be men. By night the desperate knocks on her door of slaves cutting loose, with bullet wounds and dog bites, and she stitching them up to the rhythm of soldiers tramping outside.

And at times of her choosing, the discreet knock of a lover sworn to keep the tales.

As the woman ages, she wants her own space to think and to be. She weaves around her stories of magic and bewilderment. There are sightings of her in meadows coaxing flowers to bloom, on hillsides whispering to birds, and by cemeteries communing with the dead—and sometimes of her feet not touching the ground as she moves.

People let her alone except on days set aside for healing, when they leave their gratitude as fruit or provisions, coin or cloth at her door.

On nights when the moon is full, the Old Woman casts her offerings into the sea—fish and crabs and flowers—and summons the guardians of the deep. They rise to the surface, their wing spans as wide as billowing sails, and tell her their knowings, the moods of the waves, and the terms of their trade—after shipwrecks the Old Woman will claim the living, and secure in the caverns of the sea are the dead and their tellings.

And so the Old Woman walks the rocks after each storm collecting lives.

And one day finds the Captain.

V.

On a night when the moon has retired to change faces, at a deserted beach near Point-a-Pierre on the island that hurricanes shun the Captain rows cargo from ship to shore. This is not unusual. The Captain bears risks to shield her crew.

Yet this time it's not just a matter of guns and their seasons.

At dawn on a plantation wreathed in humidity and redolent with sweat and despair the slaves revolt. At first there is no whisper of weapons, only an entreaty to justice, the right to be treated as human. But in this history that right has always been weighted. The master refuses. The soldiers duly approach. The rebels run. Someone fires. The troops respond. Someone falls. Some rebels race into the woods. The soldiers follow. To distract them someone breaks from the encircling. The soldiers fire. The figure stumbles, picks up, and drags limping into the sea. The waves redden. The figure swims. Blood trails. The figure is brave. But the body has its limits. The soldiers watch it sink.

A gift, to be cherished, must be passed on.

The Rebel wakes to gently rocking waves, bandages and instruments bloody in a bowl. The Captain sits by her, watching. The Captain smiles and looks away. The Rebel is confused. As the pain dulled by rum and coca recedes, the Rebel begins to understand. She tells the Captain a story:

In a great house in the Naparimas there lived a girl. She had all a child could desire— loving parents, adoring siblings, a caring governess. One day when she was six years old she wandered away into the cane fields by her home. She saw a whip in a hand as black as hers. It descended on backs as black as her siblings'. The governess found her frightened but would not answer her whys. The memory was etched like grooves ground in rock by the sea. Her anger grew with her at everyone telling her leave things be. Nearing womanhood, with proposals of marriage circling, a slave girl friend helped her run away. But this was not enough. She bound her breasts and clipped short her hair.

A man always gets away with more than a woman.

In Port of Spain, an accounts clerk in the Governor's employ took on a black assistant. The youth was bright and mischievous, quick to learn and laughter. A sergeant of the Governor's guard, a free black, acquired a drinking buddy in exchange for swordplay and the knowledge of guns. Keeping company with the port's prostitutes and rag pickers the youth collected stories unfit for respectable folk. One day a slave who had rebelled against his master was held in the Governor's prison. Next day his cell was empty. The soldiers were flummoxed. The prostitutes hid a man until he caught ship. He was not their client. Three guards were flogged for being remiss. The youth commiserated with the soldier friend. And went out into the night with a smile.

The ball of twine began to form.

The Captain listens. And touches the Rebel's face.

The Rebel drifts into sleep, her heart anchored.

VI.

It is said of the old woman that she had two sons. Their growing up is a mystery as none could recall them as children. She put it about that they had gone travelling at a very young age and returned to her as grown men. There is some prior knowledge of the elder as a ship's captain who on days home assists the old woman with her healing work. The younger has a slight limp, the result of misadventure with colonial authority on another island.

In the years following Emancipation, the elder acquires apprentices, girls and boys, to train in the sciences of sailing and reading the night sky. The younger gains repute in town as an educator, and advocate of self-rule. And each weekend returns to the house on the cliff.

The house keeps its secrets.

The Captain watches for evenings when the breeze is gentle and the air without clouds. Then she takes the Rebel out in a small boat.

When the last splinter of sun has conceded to darkness and whorls of distant light mantle the sky, their arms around each other they watch: in the hours between midnight and the dawn the sea draws down the stars; not all, but enough to drape the waves with luminescence.

BOOK REVIEWS

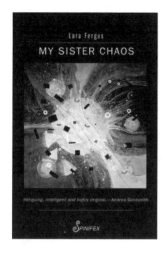

My Sister Chaos by **Lara Fergus.**
Spinifex Press, 2011.
204 pages, $15.00.

Reviewed by Joan Nestle

O*n the ragged rocks off Christmas Island, forty-eight children, women and men, desperately seeking refuge from their war-torn countries, drown in full sight of their new geography. "The boats" are a regular theme of this country in which I now live, the boats and the unwanted lives they contain. Politicians win elections based on who is toughest on "illegal arrivals."* Joan Nestle

What makes *My Sister Chaos* by Lara Fergus so compelling is that her characters, abstract and yet so known, metaphorical and yet so real, pull us profoundly into the dilemmas of displacement, psychological and physical, that mark our days. As Edward Said writes, "the 20th century [and now the 21st] has launched an age of unprecedented mass displacements" (*Reflections on Exile and Other Literary and Cultural Essays*, Granta Books, London, 2000). In this her first novel, Lara Fergus stunningly captures the disintegration of meaning facing so many in the world today as countries collapse into partisan camps, maps are redrawn, and citizens become fugitives. What happens to women who love women when they become part of the dissolution of national homes? As Fergus explains in a press release, "I've been privileged to meet some extraordinary women who have survived events and experiences that nobody should have to—and who have then had to deal with learning to live in a new country, with a new language and customs, and often without the people they love. Hearing their stories influenced how I wrote, *My Sister Chaos.*"

Unknowable and yet made known to us by their emotional and behavioral peculiarities, twin sisters, separated by the chaos of civil war, reunite in a house in an unnamed "safer" country which feels much like Australia. Quickly, sadly, the reader fills in the missing nouns—so many to choose from, so accustomed we have become to the images and stories of broken towns and back-bent refugees. This tension between Kafkaesque universality and our own certainty of detail is one mark of Fergus's narrative gift; so little usual details are given, and yet as we enter that shared house every day and night, we learn all we need to know and sometimes more then we can bear. This is a novel on one level about how two sisters, one of whom is a lesbian, struggle to recreate a center of being when their losses have literally wiped them off the map. "Countries are not mine and I am not theirs."

Like the Cook and the Carpenter in June Arnold's 1970 novel, the two sisters are known by their work and their passions, the mapmaker and the artist. Forced to share a space, their different world views, sharpened by extreme loss, clash and further separate, the artist needing the possibilities of the unmeasured, the impressions of beauty, one of the sources of chaos in the novel, the cartographer needing control over the very minutiae of her surroundings, mapping absence as well as presence.

"You will not elude me. I will measure your every dimension. I will trace your smallest lines. I will undo you from the inside. You will feel it like waves running across your floorboards, you will feel it like water rising through your walls, you will feel it like a sudden disorientation, you will wonder what happened to your foundations."

Fergus has said that what she was interested in doing in this novel was "looking at the similarities or patterns in how power operates," the malicious power of exclusion and discrimination as well as the power, I would add, of resistance. Fergus is an interesting writer who likes patterns; chapter openings sound like variations on a theme, echoing each other like some French poetic forms. Thus, the author too is part of the push and pull of disintegration and reestablishment of form that holds this novel together. Sturdy conventions of metaphors of cartography, mathematics, and musical tropes are pushed to their limits under the stress of loss. How do we recreate meaning? What code breaking skills do we need when political chaos wipes away the known and flight into uncertainty becomes a necessity? How do we find a way back into the belief that any kind of hope is possible, that even when all the boundaries have shifted and no amount of exerted control will bring back what has been lost we can find the contours of possibilities? As one of the sisters says in the novel, "The least powerful make the best cartographers. For us it is essential that we know where we are in relation to everyone else. This is not necessary for those who have the power to be at home, for whom the whole world is home."

I do not want to reveal the happenings of the novel in any greater depth—these are for you to discover— but Lara Fergus has extended the meaning of the "lesbian novel" by taking on her time, her knowledge of dislocations as they have affected so many—7.6 million people newly displaced as of June 20, 2013—and creating a fierce narrative method for her characters' attempt to hold on to meaning. Once you enter the world of *My Sister Chaos* you will always be aware of how much we count on maps of all kinds as being reliable indicators of the social contract that makes living together possible and how absurd a desire this is in such a world as ours. And yet, this novel ends with a hard won hope, and in its journey gives us a moments of women-centered community and tenderness. When the two sisters join forces, first destruction and then the possibility of light. *My Sister Chaos* is a gripping novel that is stylistically brilliant and thematically crucial.

Sister Chaos, published by Spinifex Press, 2010, Australia's award-winning feminist press, www.Spinifexpress.com.au

I want to thank the women of Spinifex for drawing our attention to this novel and to the many other fine international writings they have sent out into the world: *Goja: An Autobiographical Myth* by Suniti Namjoshi; *Love Upon the Chopping Board* by Marou Izumo and Claire Maree; *MoebiusTrip: Digressions from India's Highways* by Giti Thadani; *Remember the Tarantella* by Finola Moorhead; *Cow* by Susan Hawthorne; *Bite Your Tongue* by Francesca Rendle-Short; and *Cowrie* and *Song of the Selkies* by Cathie Dunsford.

Lesbian Marriage: A Sex Survival Kit by **Kim Chernin** and **Renate Stendhal.** www.lesbiansexsurvival.com, 2014. Paperback, $15.95 - 162 pages.

Reviewed by Kathleen DeBold

Experienced dykes know that great sex is about situations, not positions. One situation in which more and more women-loving-women find themselves is marriage. Of course, if you will be outraged that the authors use *Lesbian marriage* as the organizing principle for a book addressing *long-term Lesbian relationships*, **Lesbian Marriage: A Sex Survival Kit** is not the book for you.

If you are okay with that framing and seek commonsense guidance to keep sex and romance alive, the thoughtful advice and handy self-help tools in this playful work can help you understand and meet the challenges—sexual and otherwise—inherent in long-term relationships between women. The thoughtful and talented team of Kim Chernin (*Sex and Other Sacred Games, In My Mother's House, My Life as a Boy*) and Renate Stendahl (*True Secrets of Lesbian Desire, Gertrude Stein in Words and Pictures*) keep you engaged with their fact-based yet deeply intuitive approach to sharing love and life.

For lesbian-feminists, the contents of the book are less important than the context—lesbians providing loving assistance to sister lesbians about lesbian love. My long-term (forty years) partner and I often bemoan how assimilation and co-option have led to the detraditionalization of Lesbian folkways and Lesbian folk wisdom (we call this wistful whining "geezering"). Gone are the bars, bookstores, festivals, potlucks, and other community events where lesbians of different ages and cultural backgrounds could meet, interact, and learn from each other. Also in increasingly short supply are self-help books by, for, and about Lesbians and *any* books that explore the sexuality of older lesbians.

By creating this work, generously sharing their own experiences as long-term lovers/partners/collaborators—and now married spouses—and including engaging dialogues with a variety of other long-term couples, plus the very lesbian-y artwork by Joey Hachtman, Chernin and Stendahl provide a sense of the caring, connected Lesbian community we old-timers remember (or maybe just dreamed about?).

Strong Enough to Bend by **Judith Witherow.** Clinton, MD: Twin Spirits Press (PO Box 1353, Clinton, MD 20735), 2014.
Paperback $14.95 - 164 pages.

Review by Carol Anne Douglas

What does it mean to grow up hungry? To have no running water or electricity? To have your home torched because you're Native American? To have to work in a factory? To marry young to a violent man? To develop multiple sclerosis and lupus because you grew up in a town with water contaminated by mining? (Many of the people who have lupus are women of color. Environmental racism?) To know that all of that is wrong, dead wrong. To know you need to love women. To work in the feminist movement and face discrimination there. To be determined to raise three sons to be feminists. To know that you have to write because you have so much to say.

That describes Judith Witherow, and this is her book.

But Judith can tell about these things much more eloquently than I can.

"Imagination should have been my given name," she writes. "At school I was beaten on a regular basis because of the mental escape routes I followed." "There isn't a day the memory of someone I loved and lost doesn't claw at my being at an unguarded moment." "I wish this were a story about closets and how you find your way out. The houses I was raised in didn't contain closets. Instead of closets, there were cut-down broomsticks wedged into corners." "Some women have gotten a place at the proverbial table, while others are left to endure belly-touching-backbone hunger." "During my two years of work at a sportswear factory, I witnessed two women suffer a mental breakdown. Their screams made the hair on the back of your neck stand up. Other women would carry the women out, and hardly a moment of work would be lost."

A man harassed Judith on that job, but she went to the union; two of her aunts were union officers. She won a victory over the harasser, and has never stopped fighting since—for her relatives, for her health, for other women, and for other Native Americans.

Judith tells of her love with her partner of decades, Sue Lenaerts, who helped her leave an abusive marriage and raise their sons. Their relationship has been filled with joy despite the many incredibly hard times. "Happiness misted me like the spray from a waterfall," Judith says about the day that she finally came out to her grown sons, who told her they had known for a long time that she and Sue were lovers.

Judith's writing is compelling and her story is one that all feminists should know. I am so proud to know her. How can a woman who has grown up hungry and seen her siblings hungry be generous enough to work with those of us who have always known privilege? Judith's openness to people who try to understand never ceases to amaze me.

What is it like for a Native American woman to work her ass off organizing a feminist demonstration and see the other women freak out because there's a Native American demonstration nearby? What is it like to hear that your little sister's biggest dream in life is to have all the chicken noodle soup she can eat? What is it like to have a list of serious medical problems that is so long that doctors don't want to hear it? I don't know, but Judith tries to tell us.

Spheres of Disturbance by Amy **Schutzer.**
Pasadena, CA: Arktoi Books, 2014.
Paperback $16.95. 280 pages.

Reviewed by Ellen Goldberg

I t is October 19, 1985. In a small town in upstate New York, Avery, a lesbian poet, prepares for a garage sale in her barn, getting rid of her ex-roommates' sundry abandoned possessions. Her pot-bellied pig, Charlotta, weighed down with piglets-to-be, is about to go into labor. Avery waits for her chronically-late lover, Sammy. Sammy's mother, Helen, is dying of breast cancer. Sammy has been withdrawn from Avery, her heart protected from grief in anticipation of Helen's death. Unbeknownst to Helen, her long-lost and rejecting family is driving back into her life. Helen intends to find a way out, take the reins of the dying process. Her friend Joe has offered to help Helen with her plans. Joe's sister, an art thief, his teen-aged daughter and her best friend, and his macramé-making wife, round out the cast of characters in Amy Schutzer's *Spheres of Disturbance*. This eclectic cast each take turns narrating the story.

Quirkiness in some characters enlivens the novel and prevents morbidity from creeping in. I was especially fond of and fascinated by Charlotta with her nose and belly-centric point of view, Frances, the wicked for the hell of it and teens, Darla and Ruth. They are delicious, awkward, and brilliant. I wished for more shadow and rough edge to Avery; she functions more like a window to see others than a full-blown complex woman.

Like Schutzer's previous novel, *Undertow* (Calyx Books, 2000), the prose of *Spheres of Disturbance* is at times luminous and at other times wryly humorous. Language that is lushly metaphoric butts against the nitty-gritty: *"She would like to run away from her body. Leave it behind hanging in her closet. Not a bad dress for most of her life."* (p. 119) Period detail from 1985 provides a rich grounded texture. For example, on the tables, Avery *"pieces together...beaded fringe pocketbooks...Candyland...bongos...She comes across several stashes of old pot in film canisters."* (p.43) The story is richly plotted with plenty of twists, some suspense and charming comic scenes, especially with Charlotta. *Spheres of Disturbances* entertains as it provokes.

Character's eccentricities mirror each other: Avery with her pig pet mirrors Frances with her pet Elvis. Marjorie with her macramé echoes daughter Darla making a *papier mâché* bust of Abe Lincoln. Joe and Frances father's death informs and contrasts with Helen's impending death. In a central plot poet, birth and death unfold simultaneously, connecting one to the other.

Schutzer weaves interdependence throughout the book: mother and daughter, lover and lover, and the connections of family. Whether we like it or not, these interdependencies persist, shaping us beyond our knowing.

Interweaving of narratives and cinematic turns carry the reader through Schutzer's journey of exploring what happens to humans when someone close is dying. Reactions streak from heartbreak and compassion to self-centered rage: how to make death stop, how to make peace, how to settle scores, how to be with the reality of death, how to go on with life while our loved one is dying. The pressure of the novel's frame in a single day crystallizes the emotions that accompany death. As the characters are drawn like moths to the flame of Helen's death, they are also drawn to each other. Life and love, accompanied by wild women's down-home country music, intensify at a woodstove-heated garage sale amid the crowd's fevered shopping.

In *Spheres of Disturbance*, Schutzer accomplishes what I long for in art with lesbian characters—characters engaged with life, death, work, family—and gaining wisdom by facing it all. Schutzer describes through Avery's eyes life on lesbian land: "*The Farm was rife with ritual.... It wasn't goddesses Avery needed but making sense of the ordinary*" (p. 73). Her characters keep love going through life's difficult and tragic disturbances. They slog through pain and become larger.

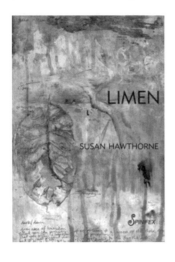

Limen by **Susan Hawthorne.**
Spinifex Press, 2013.
Paperback, $24.95. 166 pages.

Reviewed by Sarah Brooks

In psychology, the "limen" is the threshold below which one stimulus cannot be distinguished from another. In geography, the "limen" is an area of mud or silt deposited at the mouth of a river. Australian writer Susan Hawthorne's new poetic novella, *Limen*, is a story imagined within a liminal space, a story that appears to relate the experiences of two women and a dog over nine days, even as it hints at the currents that run beneath those three lives.

The narrative of *Limen* alternates between the voices of Woman 1, Woman 2, and Dog, to describe a camping trip in Queensland, Australia, on the Einasleigh River. When heavy rains swell the river and the three discover they cannot get their car out of the mud and rising water, only Dog remains calm. Woman 1 is an action-oriented scientist who observes nature. Woman 2 is a quiet worrier, tuned in to the emotions of Woman 1. Dog wants someone to throw his stick. Tension builds because we know, from the novella's beginning, that the women lost their beloved old dog a few years before, and because we are privy to both the women's inner thoughts, as well as their actions and dialogue with each other.

Hawthorne is a skilled poet, crafting alliterative lines like "wind and rain strewn/ stranded" and "sizzling in sunlight." Each word she uses matters. When two miners come walking toward the women in the mud, Dog thinks simply, "I sniff/ twenty long toes." The intimate relationship between the two women is presented quietly in lines like "where previously we had swum/ in easy nakedness." The characters' thoughts are direct and poignant, full of images that bring us to the banks of the Einasleigh, where we also wait anxiously for "life's next pounce."

Limen is more than just a story about the northern Queensland wilderness. The nine days are a "tiny crack/in our lives," "the limen . . ./ where we could/ be on both sides of time." That space, where the two women and the dog are at once freed and imprisoned by the wilderness, is a space where they are either about to exist or not. They are part of no human society; they are constrained by no rules. For the space of nine days, they are merely together, present as the cormorant or the kookaburra is present in that landscape. And even as the two women worry about how they will exit the Einasleigh safely, it is a strange calm we find in that liminal space. For the space of Hawthorne's book, we, too, can "span beingness/ like the unfinished arc/ of a bridge."

CONTRIBUTORS

Cathy Arellano is a queer Xicana writer who is haunted by and obsessed with growing up in her large, working-class Mexican family in San Francisco's Mission District. She writes poems and stories about growing up brown, coming out queer, and living "as true as I can which is kinda crooked." Her poetry and prose collection *Salvation on 24th Street* will be published by Korima Press in 2014.

Naina Ayya creates drawings and mixed media artworks. By contrasting the division between the realm of memory and the realm of experience, Ayya absorbs the tradition of remembrance art into daily practice. This personal revival of a past tradition is important as an act of meditation. Her 2013 "Diver" series explores a woman's body in the acts of swimming or diving. The body is viewed from the perspective of the female inner eye, observing the physicality of the body and beyond to a meditative spiritual realm, collapsing physical distance and boundaries. Ayya's art education includes art classes in public schools and a community arts center in the U.S. Early influences include children's book illustrations and the saturated colors of her mother's saris. Based in San Francisco, she is currently studying art at the University of California–Berkeley Extension.

Kathleen DeBold is a member of the *Sinister Wisdom* board of directors.

Dovey Dee was born in southern Louisiana and raised in southern California. She studied fine arts and has made paintings, sculpture, and furniture for a long time. Dee graduated from Scripps College (one of the last all women's colleges in the U.S.) in 1983 and from Claremont Graduate University in 1985. She also has a penchant for machine design and spatial problem solving, and this talent has provided her with income when art didn't. In 2000 Dee migrated to Australia. Currently when not making paintings or furniture, she works for the Australian Bureau of Meteorology as a spatial data engineer, helping to build the national hydrologic spatial database.

From 1973 to 2008, **Carol Anne Douglas** was a member of the collective that edited the feminist news journal *off our backs*. She has written a book on feminist theory, *Love and Politics: Radical Feminist and Lesbian Theories*. She belongs to Old Lesbians Organizing for Change (OLOC) and is a founding member of the Washington Metropolitan Area chapter of OLOC. She is now writing fiction and plays. Visit her website at www.carolannedouglas.com.

Lara Fergus grew up in the western suburbs of Sydney and gave up a science degree to become a contemporary dancer until injury ended that career. She spent several years living overseas, mostly in France. In that time she completed degrees in writing, women's studies, and international law, and worked with various advocacy organizations, including those for newly arrived immigrant and refugee women. She currently works for the Victorian government on policy to prevent violence against women. She lives in Melbourne with her partner Maryse, writes before she works, and dances on the weekends.

Mariam Gagoshashvili is a queer feminist from Tbilisi, Georgia. Currently she lives in San Francisco and works at the Global Fund for Women as a program officer for Europe and central Asia. Before joining the Global Fund for Women, Mariam worked as a program coordinator at the Women's Fund for Georgia in southwest Asia. She serves as an advisor for two women's funds: The Young Feminist Fund (FRIDA) and the Urgent Action Fund for Women's Human Rights. Mariam has also been involved in grassroots feminist and LGBTQI activism. She has lectured for the gender studies master's program at Tbilisi State University and cofounded the Independent Group of Feminists, an autonomous activist collective run by young women in Georgia.

Xi'an Glynn received her MA in English and communication from SUNY–Potsdam in 2011. She is a health educator with Iris House, working extensively with the LGBT population. She is also a business development associate, content producer, and production assistant for the independent film company Clarendon Enterprises and CEI Media Partners. In her early career, she had the opportunity to intern for many successful companies and organizations including the music video department of Atlantic Records, Wendy Williams of 107.5 FM WBLS, and BronxNet Television. For the past ten years she has been a member of African Ancestral Lesbians United for Social Change (AALUSC) and she currently is a member of their advisory board. In the winter of 2013, Xi'an was featured in a photography project called "What Dyke Looks Like." Xi'an loves to sing, dance, and write.

Samar Habib is an associate researcher in the Center for Gender Studies at the School of Oriental and African Studies, the University of London. She is the author of the novels *Roghum and Najda: A Novel* (Oracle Releasing, Los Angeles, 2012) and *A Tree Like Rain* (Nebula Press, Sydney, 2005). Her academic titles include *Female Homosexuality in the Middle East* (Routledge, New York, 2007) and *Islam and Homosexuality* (2 vols, Praeger, Westport, CT, 2010), among others.

Emerging from a dysfunctional 1970s childhood into a variety of practical jobs in her teens, **Janet Jones** emerged from a long heterosexual experimental "phase," found her way back into education and out into her butch lesbian identity. With feminist politics, community theater, visual expression, creative writing and lots of work and activism, life moved forward. Halfway through her thirties, the most common degenerative disease neurological condition affecting women, Multiple Sclerosis, emerged, and five years into a community development and food policy role, her life changed. Disability and medical retirement necessitated a new creative direction and ten years on, a different life has taken shape. Her short film "Butch Losses: Butch Identity and Disability" has been screened at two Lesbian Lives Conferences and shown to social work students.

Bonnilee Kaufman is a learning disabilities specialist for the California community colleges. She received a partial scholarship to the Lambda Literary Foundation's writing retreat for emerging voices (2012). Her poetry has been included in two anthologies: *Ghosts of the Holocaust: An Anthology of Poetry* by the Second Generation (Stewart J. **Florsheim and Gerald Stern** (editors), Wayne State University Press, Indiana, 1989) and *Milk and Honey—A Celebration of Jewish Lesbian Poetry* (Julie R. Enszer (editor), Midsummer Night's Press, Spain, 2011).

khulud khamis is a Palestinian feminist writer, born to a Slovak mother and a Palestinian father. Growing up in two countries and between two cultures, her identity is composed of both and her multicultural background affects her writing. She currently lives in Haifa with her daughter. Her first novel, *Haifa Fragments*, is scheduled to be published around October 2014 by the Australia-based Spinifex Press. In 2003, khulud received the Lis Miller Award for Literary Achievements, from the Faculty of Humanities, Haifa University. Several of her non-fiction articles appeared on the Peace X Peace website (http://www.peacexpeace.org/). khulud holds a master's degree in English literature from the University of Haifa and works in the field of social change organizations. She is a feminist activist and member of the feminist organization Isha L'Isha–Haifa Feminist Center. In her fiction, poetry, and nonfiction, khulud deals with political and social issues such as identity, belonging, racism and discrimination, art as political resistance, and issues affecting women and the LGBTQI community, all from a feminist perspective. khulud publishes some of her writings on her blog at: ww.haifafieldnotes.blogspot.com.

Ronna Magy is a Los Angeles-based writer of short story, memoir and poetry. Her recent work appears in: *Up, Do: Flash Fiction by Women Writers, Trivia: Voice of Feminism, MuseWrite, Where Thy Dark Eye Glances: Queering E. A. Poe, Southern Women's Review,* and *Lady Business: a Celebration of Lesbian poetry.* She is the author of several English as a Second Language textbooks.

Terry Martin is an English professor at Central Washington University. She has published over two hundred and fifty poems, articles, and essays, and has edited journals, books, and anthologies. Her second book of poems, *The Secret Language of Women,* was published by Blue Begonia Press in 2006. She lives in Yakima, Washington—the fruit bowl of the nation.

Yael Mishali is a Mizrahi femme writer and activist. Her PhD examines butch-femme culture and legacy, questions of marginal autobiography and experience, and queer femininity. Her current postdoctoral research focuses on Mizrahi queers analyzing intersections of gender, sexuality, ethnicity, and class. Yael is a lecturer in gender studies programs both at Tel Aviv University and at Ben Gurion University of the Negev, Israel. She is also active in various feminist and queer groups in Tel Aviv, writes poetry, and performs Mizrahi FtF drag.

Lepa Mladjenovic is a feminist lesbian activist who has spent many years working as a feminist counselor for women who have suffered the trauma of male violence in Serbia, Croatia, Bosnia, Herzegovina, and Kyrgyzstan. For over thirty years Lepa has been engaged in founding groups that try to mitigate the pain of women in violent settings as well as create safe spaces for lesbians to organize and discuss their challenges. In 1990, Lepa founded Arkadia, a lesbian and gay group; in 1993, she cofounded the Autonomous Women's Center Against Sexual Violence where she worked as a counselor and coordinator; and in 1995 she cofounded Labrys, an organization for Lesbian Human Rights. An antiwar activist, since 1991 she has been a member of Women in Black Against War, a feminist antifascist group in Belgrade, Serbia. Lately she has been engaged writing about lesbians in the peace movement and during war. In 1994 she received the Filipa da Souza Award from the International Gay and Lesbian Human Rights Commission and in 2013 she received the Anne Klein Award for her work on women's rights and lesbian activism.

Sue Carroll Moore (SMoore), LCSW, ASCAP, is a psychotherapist, poet, and playwright, who was born, raised, and educated in the Midwest. She is a cofounder of Life Mission Associates, a program to help people find their purpose in life. A significant part of her life mission is lesbian political activism. She founded *Lavender Woman* in Chicago in 1971 and was the director of Lesbian Central in Los Angeles, 1984–85. She founded Westside Women Over 40 in 1989. She has been pondering the topic of lesbians and exile ever since she moved in 2006 to be with her German partner in Saarbruecken, a tough, challenging and uncomfortable experience, but in a way, she writes, lesbians are in emotional exile from the get go, always living in 'another country.'

Ghaida Moussa is a scholar, educator and DJ, who is passionately drawn to creative articulations of resistance, identity, memory, and space. She holds a bidisciplinary master's degree in international development and global studies and women's studies from the University of Ottawa. Her master's thesis, "Narrative (sub) Versions: How Queer Palestinian Womyn 'Queer' Palestinian Identity," focuses on narrative and creative resistance by queer Palestinian womyn in response to national, colonial, and neocolonial mainstream oppressive discourses. She is currently undertaking her PhD in social and political thought at York University in Toronto, Canada, where she is attempting to make sense of the interactions between home and our collective relationship with the dead, relying heavily on notions of haunting, mourning, displacement, violence, and belonging. In the past couple of years, she has been devoted to translating anticolonial imaginations onto dance floors, thinking through "home" in the cracks between anchored locations and collective memory, and practicing pedagogy from the heart in the classroom and in alternate spaces of education. She is the coeditor of *Min Fami: Arab Feminist Reflections on Identity, Space, and Resistance*, an anthology published by Inanna Publications in March 2014.

Joan Nestle was born in the Bronx in 1940 and spent most of her life in New York City, where, in 1958, she entered public lesbian life in the bars of Greenwich Village. She taught writing in the SEEK Program at Queens College from 1965 to 1990. In 1974 she cofounded the Lesbian Herstory Archives which still thrives today in its Brooklyn home. Her own provinciality ended, she hopes, when she moved to Melbourne, Australia, in 2002 to be with her lover, Dianne Otto. At seventy-three Nestle is most grateful when she is forced to see with new eyes that which she thought she knew. She is the author of *A Restricted Country* (Cleis Press, San Francisco, 2003, first published Firebrand Press, Ithaca N.Y., 1987) and *A Fragile Union* (Cleis Press, San Francisco, 1998) and editor of seven other books exploring the lesbian body and imagination. For her most recent writing, see http://Joannestle.com.

Jeanine Olsen is an artist who creates narratives that are fantastical and absurd while rooted in mythology, anxieties, and ritual. Her work is mainly performance, installation, and photographic, but she will do something different if it suits her needs. She is committed to the ethics and practices of feminist and queer thought, and has learned a precious, unquantifiable amount from her elders who have embodied this far longer than she has been alive. Olson is an assistant professor at Parsons the New School for Design, see http://www.jeanineolsen.com.

Doreen Perrine is a writer, artist, and art teacher who came out later in life with something to express in words, that for the first time, she couldn't say in paint. Doreen has published two novels through Bedazzled Ink Publishing Company and her third novel was released in July 2014. One of Doreen's short stories was recently selected as a finalist in South African *Bloody Parchment Horrorfest* and her short stories and two novellas have been published in numerous anthologies, literary journals, and e-zines. Her play series, *Faces...Voices*, which addresses hate crimes, has been performed throughout New York City. Doreen resides in the Hudson Valley region of New York and her website address is http://doreenperrine.tripod.com/

Grace Poore (gracepoore), from Malaysia, has been the regional coordinator for Asia and the Pacific Islands at the International Gay and Lesbian Human Rights Commission (IGLHRC) since 2007. She oversees multicountry human rights documentation and advocacy projects in Asia and conducts training on human rights documentation. She cowrote the video, "Courage Unfolds," about the Yogyakarta Principles and LGBT activism in Asia. Her other two documentary films, *Voices Heard Sisters Unseen* and *The Children We Sacrifice*, have been viewed in eighteen countries. Poore has been published in several anthologies, including *Body Evidence: Intimate Violence against South Asian Women in America* (Shamita Das Dasgupta, ed., Rutgers University Press, New Brunswick, N.J., 2007), *A Patchwork Shawl: Chronicles of South Asian Women in America* (Shamita Das Dasgupta, ed., Rutgers University Press, New Brunswick, N.J., 1998) and *Our Feet Walk the Sky: Women of the South Asian Diaspora* (The Women of South Asian Descent Collective, ed., Aunt Lute Books, San Francisco, 1993); in journals, including *Sinister Wisdom 47, Conditions 13,* and *Trikone*. She co-authored the 2010 report, *Shattered Lives: Homicides, Domestic Violence and Asian Families* (U.S. Asian and Pacific Islander Institute on Domestic Violence). More recently, she is a contributor to online journals such as the *Huffington Post* and *The New Civil Rights Movement.*

Igballe (Igo) Rogova and the women of the Kosovo Women's Network know that viable and fruitful postconflict reconciliation and reconstruction must be built both around women and in partnership with the women's movement. Igballe was an activist before the war, during the war, and after the war. In 1993, she was founder of the rural women's group Motrat Qirizi when it meant walking to the most remote places in the mountains to gather women together so they would be able collectively to recognize their own power for the first time. In 1999 she founded and currently serves as the executive director of Kosovo's Women's Network with 104 women's organizations. Igballe is a leading figure in the women's movement and was awarded the Woman of the Year Award by the international Network of Women's Organizations. Since 2006 she has been the key initiator behind the establishment and initiatives of the Women's Peace Coalition that put together the Kosovo Women's Network and the Women in Black Network Serbia in an independent citizens' initiative founded on women's solidarity that crosses divisions of ethnicity, religion, and state borders.

Urška Sterle is award winning author of short fiction, translator, video artist and performer. For her debut, a collection of short stories *Vrsta za kosilo* (Queuing for lunch), published by SKUC-Vizibilija, Ljubljana, 2006, she was nominated for the award Fabula for best collection of short fiction in Slovene literature in 2007. The same year she won Zlata ptica, an award for modern art. Her book of short stories *Konstantno vojno stanje* (Constant Warfare) was published in December 2010 (SKUC-Vizibilija). Apart from her writing and translating (Sarah Schulman, Djuna Barnes, Audre Lorde) she does political stand-up comedy and other performances including touring with her one woman show,

"Lezbicne pravljice, pravljice za lezbijke" (Lesbian Fairytales, Fairytales for Lesbians).

Yasmin Tambiah grew up in Sri Lanka and lived there before and during the war years. She has spent long periods of her adult life in the U.S. and Australia, with stints in Trinidad, India, the U.K. and Spain. Trained as a European medievalist she now researches issues at the crossing points of law, gender, ethnicity, sexuality, and militarization in postcolonial states, and also works in research management. Her creative writing has appeared, among others, in *Conditions* (New York), *Options* (Colombo), *Nethra* (Colombo) and *ZineWest* (Sydney), as well as in anthologies edited by Joan Nestle and by Yasmine Gooneratne. She has won awards for writing from the Astraea Lesbian Foundation in New York and, most recently, from ZineWest in Sydney.

Jean Taylor has been writing and publishing her own work for well over thirty years. Her latest books are *Brazen Hussies: A History of Radical Activism in the Women's Liberation Movement in Victoria 1970–1979* (Melbourne: Dyke Books Inc., 1990) and *Stroppy Dykes: Radical Lesbian Feminist Activism in Victoria During the 1980s* (Melbourne: Dyke Books, Inc., 2012). She is currently working on *Lesbians Ignite in Victoria in the 1990s.*

Natasa Velikonja, born in Nova Gorica, Slovenia, in 1967, has been living in Ljubljana, the capital, since 1986 where she now does her ground breaking cultural, scientific and artistic work. A sociologist, poet, translator, and essay writer who has published four poetry collections: *Abonma* [Subscriptions], (SKUC, 1994)—the first lesbian book of poetry in the Slovene language, *Zeja* [Thirst], (SKUC, 1999), and *Plevel* [Weeds], (SKUC, 2004) and *Poljub Ogledala* [The Kiss of the Mirror], (SKUC, 2007). From 1994 on, Natasa has been a pioneering gay and lesbian activist in Slovenia first in the lesbian and gay Roza Club and since 1997, in the lesbian group, LL. In 1995, she edited the first thematic issue of *Gay and*

and Lesbian Studies in Slovenia; from 1997 on she has been the editor of the cultural, political journal, *Lesbo*. In 2000, Velikonja edited *The Selected Bibliography of Gay and Lesbian Literature in the Slovene Language* and in 2004, the anthology, *20 Years of the Gay and Lesbian Movement in Slovenia*. One of her latest books is *The Lesbian Bar* (Lezbicni Bar, 2011). Her translations include work by Monique Wittig, Lillian Faderman, Teresa de Lauretis, Elizabeth Lapkovsky Kennedy, Madeline Davis and Colette. In her spare time, Velikonja is the founder and coordinator of the Lesbian Library and Archives in Ljubljana. (Editors' Note: We have reduced three pages of Velikonja's cultural work to this paragraph; the superlatives are ours, the years of dedication are Natasa's.)

Voltrina Williams, LMSW, is a developing author who works in the field of social services. She holds a bachelor's degree from Georgia State University and a master's degree from the University of South Carolina. In a burst of premenopausal creativity, Ms. Williams has just completed her first women's literary fiction titled, *The Replacements*. She has been previously published in *Kalyani Magazine* and is a Money for Women/Barbara Deming grant recipient.

Audrey Yue is associate professor in cultural studies at the University of Melbourne, Australia. Her most recent publications are *Sinophone Cinemas* (Palgrave MacMillan, Melbourne, 2014), *Queer Singapore: Illiberal Citizenship and Mediated Cultures* (Hong Kong University Press, Hong Kong, 2012). She is completing a monograph on queer Asian migration to Australia.

'Sexual orientation and gender identity and the protection of forced migrants'

Free online and in print...

Issue 42 of Forced Migration Review includes 26 articles on the abuse of rights of forced migrants who identify as lesbian, gay, bisexual, transgender or intersex.

Around the world, people face abuse, arbitrary arrest, extortion, violence, severe discrimination and lack of official protection because of their sexual orientation and/or gender identity. Authors discuss both the challenges faced and examples of good practice in securing protection for LGBTI forced migrants.

Available online and in print in English, French, Spanish and Arabic. Individual articles are online in pdf, html and (in English) audio/MP3 formats. To access online and/or request print copies, please visit: www.fmreview.org/sogi

Forced Migration Review is published by the Refugee Studies Centre at the University of Oxford.

FORCED MIGRATION review

Issue 42
April 2013

Sexual orientation and gender identity and the protection of forced migrants

FOR FREE DISTRIBUTION ONLY   UNIVERSITY OF OXFORD   REFUGEE STUDIES CENTRE

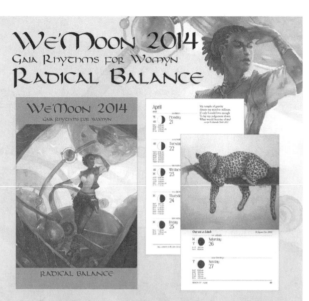

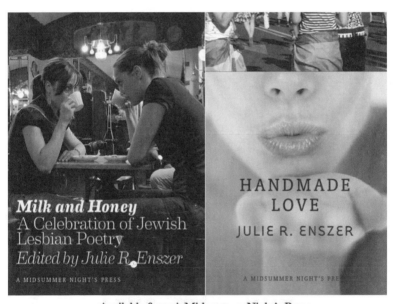

Sinister Wisdom **Back Issues Available**

*Available on audio tape

Back issues are $6.00 unless noted plus $2.00 Shipping & Handling for 1st issue; $1.00 for each additional issue. Order online at www.sinisterwisdom.org

Or mail check or money order to:
Sinister Wisdom
PO Box 3252
Berkeley, CA 94703